Border Ransom

Pat Carr

TCU Press
Fort Worth, Texas

Border Ransom

by Pat Carr

Library of Congress Cataloging-in-Publication Data

Carr, Pat M., 1932-
    Border ransom / by Pat Carr.-- 1st ed.
        p. cm.
    Summary: When her parents die in the influenza epidemic, fif-
teen-year-old Cooper goes to live with her grandparents in El Paso,
where she finds that her grandmother is remote and childlike and
her grandfather is trafficking in stolen antiques and running guns to
Pancho Villa and his Mexican revolutionaries.
    ISBN-13: 978-0-87565-332-7 (alk. paper)
    ISBN-10: 0-87565-332-4 (alk. paper)
    [1. Orphans--Fiction. 2. Grandparents--Fiction. 3. Villa,
Pancho, 1878-1923--Fiction. 4. Mexico--History--Revolution, 1910-
1920--Fiction. 5. El Paso (Tex.)--History--20th century--Fiction.] I.
Title.
    PZ7.C22985Bor 2006
    [Fic]--dc22

                                                2006002210

                        TCU Press
                    P. O. Box 298300
                   Fort Worth, TX 76129
                      817-257-7822
                  http://www.prs.tcu.edu
               To order books: 1-800-826-8911

                     Printed in Canada

            Designed by Barbara Mathews Whitehead

Border Ransom

1

THE SECOND I KNOTTED the ribbon of Mama's hat under my chin and stepped off the train onto the platform I knew everything was wrong.

Maybe I knew because, as the train jolted to a stop in the El Paso station and I dragged my trunk through the vestibule between the cars, I caught the hard glitter of barbed wire strung along the banks of the Rio Grande.

Or maybe I knew because my grandfather sat, alone, in a wagon, when he should have been behind the wheel of a brand new 1914 Packard with my grandmother, wrapped in a fur coat, beside him in the passenger seat. I wasn't dumb enough to expect my grandmother to be wearing Russian mink in a southwest August, but all the way from New Orleans, I'd imagined my grandparents waiting for me together in an elegant, up-to-date motorcar. Looking for me, just the way they'd both stared at the camera in the last photo they'd sent my mother and father for Christmas.

Or maybe the panic, the terror actually, that leapt around in my skull came from the pounding certainty that whatever happened now, I had nowhere else to go.

"Davis?" my grandfather said as if I might not have noticed him in his dark suit there below the platform, watching from beneath the brim of a black slouch hat. Or as if he didn't quite recognize me from the photograph my parents had mailed to El Paso the Easter before they'd died.

My grandfather spoke as quietly as the steam huffing from the train engine, but I could tell that he was used to being listened to no matter how softly he spoke. I also knew from my father, his only child, that he considered raising his voice in public a lower-class sort of thing, which no American descendant of a minor English lord should do.

So I didn't call back as I bounced my trunk down the hobnailed iron train steps and let it thud onto the wooden platform.

Dozens of other passengers climbed down from the train around me and hurried toward the red brick depot to flee the sun, but my grandfather didn't budge. He didn't move to help me drag the trunk across the rough planks even though I thought that was something a gentleman—especially an American descendant of English aristocracy—should do.

"I've called myself 'Cooper,' not 'Davis' since I was five," I said evenly as the trunk and I reached the edge of the platform.

My grandfather started and glanced toward the curve-topped trunk that had been Papa's and that now held everything I owned. Since I concluded he had no intention of hugging me on our first ever meeting, I let myself examine him.

The Christmas photo showed his gray hair, but in person, he seemed even older, and the creases across his forehead, the crevices swooping toward his prominent jaw gave him the appearance of some Old Testament prophet. He also had a sun-burned face that I assumed came from living in the desert. He hadn't taken off his hat, but since few men back home tipped their hats to me, I decided that he, too, probably still thought of me as a child.

He kept studying the trunk while he said, "Is that all you brought?"

I nodded silently—forcing him to look up.

As his gray eyes met mine, however, I couldn't control the tightening in my throat, and this time I glanced away.

I adjusted the beaded purse on my arm, but just as I was about to topple the trunk into the wagon by myself, my grandfather finally stood up and reached for the handle.

He was also shorter than I'd imagined, and he didn't stand any taller than I did as he grabbed the trunk and swung it off the platform.

It landed neatly in the wagon bed, and my grandfather took my gloved hand and helped me down into the wagon.

His fingers clamped hard over mine, and in only the few seconds it took me to descend to the wooden seat, balance myself in my Sunday lace-up patent boots, and then step to the wagon floor, my hand had started to go dead.

Fortunately, as soon as he released my fingers, I could square my shoulders and try to get my breath in the heat.

I made myself stare into his gray eyes that had glints of steel.

"Your father named you 'Davis' because it was my mother's surname," he said as he sat down. "He gave it to you at my request."

I glared at him from under the brim of the black straw hat. "I know," I said. I didn't remind him that 'Cooper' had been Mama's family surname. I also resisted saying that 'Cooper' and 'Davis' were both stupid, not proper first names at all, no matter who requested them, and certainly not anything to inflict on a baby—particularly not on a female baby. I'd be able to change 'Harrison' if I ever got married, but I was stuck with those two ridiculous Christian names for life.

I glared a moment longer and didn't explain that when I'd started school, I'd chosen to call myself the ridiculous name I disliked the least.

But as I plunked down next to him on the unpadded wagon seat, I didn't say anything else, so my grandfather either had to speak or take up the reins.

He chose the latter.

I smelled the hot wool of his suit as he lifted a whip from its holder beside the seat and cracked it above the white and brown rump of the horse.

The mottled horse responded to the snap of the whip and lunged the wagon forward while the train whistle sounded and another whoosh of steam issued from the engine. Trolley bells jangled, and car horns honked.

I didn't try to make conversation amid the noise as we passed the red brick depot, and I caught glimpses of the Rio Grande, the stucco houses, and church steeples of Juarez across the barbed wire. I also caught a glimpse, without wanting to, of the placard over the station door that said, "1208 Miles to New Orleans."

My breath stopped for a second.

But as the wagon rumbled over the graveled lot and crossed another set of tracks bordered with more fencing, my lungs started working again.

Sunlight gleamed on the wire strands and barbs, and we were jostled over the tracks and then out the gate of the railroad yard.

During the trip across Texas, I'd visualized El Paso as a thrown-together heap of adobe huts huddled around a trading post, looking as dry and forlorn as any of the little Texas towns the train had chugged through without stopping.

But when we emerged from the train yard onto a wide paved street, I realized El Paso wasn't like that at all.

Five- and six-story yellow brick buildings rose from hard-swept sidewalks, electric trolley lines centered the street, and electric streetlights hung in globed clusters from wrought iron posts on every block. Colorful signs and painted advertisements on the sides of the buildings offered everything from crystal goblets to the current models of sewing machines and the latest Fords, and I'd never seen more elegant straw hats than the ones in the millinery shop windows.

"We'll drive by the store, but we won't stop," my grandfather said as we passed the Orndorff Hotel on one side of the street and the green square of a plaza on the other. "I'll take you in tomorrow and you can start learning the business."

I had no idea what kind of business my grandfather owned, but when I'd written the letter asking if I could come, I said I'd be willing to help wherever I was needed. And since there wasn't anything I could add to that, I merely nodded.

After no more than a minute, my grandfather yanked the reins and stopped the horse while he pointed the whip toward a building with HARRISON AND ROBARTS stenciled in black letters high up on the yellow bricks. "There it is," he said.

Most buildings on the block had been painted with the names of the owners or their wares—UNEEDA BISCUIT or MILLER'S NOTIONS—and most had awnings that sheltered the storefronts. Under my grandfather's green awning, fancy gilt script spelled out ANTIQUES across the polished glass of the large front window.

So, I'd come to El Paso to learn the antique business.

In the dismay of my arrival, I couldn't focus on anything in the window, but my parents had always assured me I could learn anything, so I sat on the wagon box and I told myself that my brain would surely stop whirling by morning.

Fortunately, just then the horse clopped off again, clanging his iron shoes against the brick pavement past the Bijou Theatre and the sandwich board out front that advertised Pearl White's *Perils of Pauline.*

My grandfather frowned. "Moving pictures are a fad that won't last, but no telling how many apprentices and shop girls in the meantime will squander their entire salaries, a nickel at a time, to watch grown men and women scurry around like inebriated ants."

I knew it wasn't the time to mention that Mama, Papa, and I had gone to motion picture theatres all the time in New Orleans, so I kept quiet and watched the brown and white splotches of the horse ripple in the sunlight.

I narrowed my eyelids against the glistening horsehide while I concluded I'd never been so thirsty or so hot.

But my grandfather didn't seem to notice the heat, and since I didn't want to call attention to my own discomfort by digging in the little jet-beaded purse—which had also belonged to Mama—for a handkerchief, I let the ribbons of perspiration run unchecked down my face.

I couldn't make myself ask where we were going, so I merely sat and tried to breathe as the wagon rolled through the paved streets and turned onto a wide dirt lane.

Blocks of sturdy houses replaced the shops and bank buildings, wooden fences and wooden sidewalks replaced the streetlamps and trolley lines. We turned corner after corner until at last the horse veered into a circular driveway before a three-story stucco house and stopped beside a stone fountain.

The huge house, roofed with red tiles, plastered pale yellow, and ringed by a stand of cottonwood trees, rivaled the grand antebellum homes in New Orleans, and I realized that my grandparents were wealthy.

A spindly-legged man, dressed in a shirt, pants, and hat the color of his brown skin, banged open the door of the stables behind the house and ran across the yard. His boots crunched the gravel as he grabbed the bridle and panted, "Whoa, Raphael," even though the horse was drinking placidly from the fountain pool.

But the little man held the bridle firmly, as if Raphael would gallop away any second, while he beamed up at me. "Is this Señorita Davis, Señor Harrison?"

"She calls herself 'Cooper' now."

My grandfather replaced the whip in its holder and got down from the wagon. "Carry her trunk to the third-floor room after you put the horse away."

"Sí, Señor Harrison." He dropped the bridle and bounded to my side. He held up a palm to help me down and smiled with a row of glittering teeth. "Welcome to El Paso, Señorita Cooper. I am Tomás Iglesias. I drive for Señor Harrison. Your grandmother has been afraid you missed your train."

I knew my grandfather, standing beside the fountain, frowning in his kidskin gloves, dark wool suit and celluloid collar, must be melting. But I couldn't let the friendly driver go unanswered, so I said, "They had to stop and pull a dead bull off the tracks outside Fort Stockton, and the train was delayed."

My grandfather stepped onto the porch and into a tiny strip of shade.

"It's a good thing I didn't send you to the station, Tomás," he said over his shoulder. "Cooper might not have accepted a ride with a complete stranger."

Just then the front door opened to a woman in a floor-length black taffeta dress, and I didn't get a chance to say that actually I had accepted a ride with a complete stranger.

2

"IS THIS DAVIS AT LAST, Mr. Harrison?" The grandmother I'd never met, whose black dress might indicate she still mourned her son, stood in the doorway only a second before she disappeared back inside.

I passed the fountain and couldn't help glancing at the crystal drops splashing into the water and scattering miniature suns over the golden carp that flickered, unconcerned, through the pool. The horse, equally unconcerned, lapped his great tongue above the fish, and I wished I could pause a second and scoop up a drink along with him.

But since I couldn't, I climbed the porch steps after my grandfather.

"She's calling herself 'Cooper' now," he repeated—for what I hoped would be the last time—to my grandmother as he went into the house.

My grandmother kept deep in the shadowed entryway as she glanced after him and then looked back at me with pale blue eyes. Ringlets hugged her cheeks, every hair in perfect curls as if they'd been made of china. "You're so tall," she said extending tiny hands to me. Her dainty hands and dainty voice matched the blue ribbon around her forehead.

I couldn't tell her that Papa had said I probably didn't have my full height yet, so I murmured, "I'm fifteen."

I accepted the fact that she wasn't going to hug me either, and I took the little outstretched hands.

Every finger wore a ring, and I tried not to press too hard and gouge her with the prongs. I hadn't noticed when she'd held out her hands, but somehow as I clasped her fingers and focused on the diamond brooch at her collar, the large diamond studs in her ears, I suspected that all the rings had been set with diamonds.

She reached by me and pulled the door shut.

The sun vanished, and since I couldn't see anything, I just stood there with my gloved hands feeling much too big to be holding her bejeweled fingers.

"You must be starved, Dav—Cooper." She caught herself politely. "It was a shame you had to make this trip by yourself. But nowadays, Mr. Harrison can't leave the store except to go on buying trips."

"We stopped by the store so she could see it," my grandfather said from somewhere in the cave-like parlor. "I'll start educating her about antiques tomorrow."

He was talking about me as if I weren't standing right there.

My grandmother angled her neck toward him. "I wrote Mrs. Robarts that Davis—Cooper—" she amended again, "—is to be your new assistant." Then she explained in my direction, "Mr. Robarts and Mr. Harrison were in business together until Mr. Robarts died last year. His wife has kept the antique store in Philadelphia, and Mr. Harrison still ships the better antiques back East." A faint lisp haloed her words as she repeated, "But it was a shame you had to make the trip by yourself."

Before I could say that I preferred traveling alone so I could read, she added, "And I'm sorry we couldn't come to New Orleans for the funeral last year."

I almost let that slide, but then before I knew I was going to say it, I heard myself correcting her with, "Funerals."

I saw through the darkness that she gave her head a little bird tilt at my emphasis.

"Papa died two weeks after Mama did," I said.

I'd practiced saying the sentence for nearly ten months, but it still came out more choked than I wanted it to.

"Oh, yes," she agreed. Her agreement wasn't at all choked, and she might have been speaking about casual acquaintances as she went on, "It's a marvel you weren't carried off by the flu as well."

"Papa stayed with his congregation, and Mama stayed with him. But they sent me to Memphis with Mama's best friend, Rosalie Boudreaux, when the epidemic began."

"And it was Rosalie Boudreaux who wrote to us about your parents' deaths?"

I nodded.

"She's the one you lived with to finish high school this spring? The one who got married in February?"

I nodded again for both questions.

When she didn't follow up those queries, I was relieved. At least she hadn't asked if Rosalie's new bridegroom had been the real reason I'd fled to El Paso.

She released my hands, backed away, and gave me another long look through the gloom.

Her taffeta rustled, and she retreated another step, making me feel too pole-high for her to see all in one glance, and said in the little girl voice that was somehow fake, "Do you think Yolanda should serve the lemonade and the cucumber sandwiches now, Mr. Harrison? Don't you think this tall child should eat?"

My eyes were adjusting, and I could see dark pieces of furniture, a grand piano, couches, loveseats, armchairs, and scores of tables crammed with beaded lamps and porcelain fruit. A stucco arch to a formal dining room opened onto a massive table and a chandelier so dark that it could have dangled dusty grapes rather than crystals from its brass curlicues.

My grandfather stood beside the arch and a tapestry bell pull, and my grandmother glanced at him. "Is Tomás bringing in Cooper's things?"

"She only brought one trunk, Angelica."

He tugged the bell cord.

"What a frugal traveler you must be," she murmured as she left the dark entryway and floated into the dark parlor. "When I used to travel, I never went anywhere without a dozen steamer trunks."

She stopped in the middle of the carpet and pointed to a love seat whose murky upholstery could have been any color. "Why don't you come sit down so we can get acquainted? We'll have a little talk and a snack, and then Yolanda will show you to your room. After such a long trip, you need a good rest before dinner."

I started to say that I wasn't hungry or exhausted, that I was just hot and thirsty and not used to finding my way around rooms as black as closets, but before I said it, a dark-skinned girl—her complexion made darker by the contrasting snowiness of her maid's uniform—pushed open the swinging door of the dining room and let in a sliver of light. The gloom descended again as the door swung shut.

"Señora Harrison would like you to bring in the sandwiches now, Yolanda," my grandfather said.

The dusk made his words more subdued than ever, but I heard quite plainly that he'd issued a command.

"Sí, Señor Harrison," the girl said.

I fumbled my way down into the sunken parlor, hoping I could avoid the corners of the heavy mahogany furniture.

I managed to reach the loveseat without careening into anything or knocking anything over, and as I sat down I could tell by the feel of the cushions that the loveseat had velvet upholstery.

But I still couldn't see well enough to discern what color it was.

I pulled off my gloves and laid them beside me on Mama's purse as the girl disappeared again in the quick band of light.

"Everything is ready. Yolanda fixed the sandwiches some time ago. I hope the bread hasn't dried out." My grandmother fluttered to an armchair across from the loveseat and sank into it, rustling. "Your train was so late."

"The sandwiches will be fine, Angelica," my grandfather said. I could hear that he protected her and at the same time belittled her.

"I do hope you like cucumber sandwiches, Cooper."

Before I could excuse the delay of the train because of the dead bull, before I could add that I'd never tasted a cucumber sandwich, the swinging door reopened, and the maid bobbed across the dining room into the parlor.

In the kitchen, she'd pinned a tiny white maid's cap, shaped like a paper boat, to her coils of black hair, and despite the fact that she was no taller than my grandmother, she effortlessly balanced a huge silver tray freighted with a crystal pitcher and glasses, little cut-glass saucers, and a footed plate of sandwiches.

She wove around the bulky furniture in the semi-darkness.

"I think Yolanda is about your age, Cooper," my grandmother said.

Actually, the roundness of her cheeks and the sturdiness of her wrists beneath the cuffs of her white sleeves gave me the impression she might still have her baby fat. She might in fact be younger than I was.

"Since Cooper is new to El Paso, perhaps she can ask Yolanda what teen-aged girls do for entertainment here," my grandmother added.

She'd dropped the child-like tone, and she now matched my grandfather's disparagement. She also spoke as if neither the maid nor I were in the room. "Coming to a house that belongs to a couple of stodgy old people, she may—"

My grandfather cut her off with a snap of irritation. "Don't talk nonsense, Angelica."

She glanced toward him, and in the semidarkness, her pale eyes glinted. "I just thought that perhaps since Yolanda and Cooper are so young, they could—"

My grandfather dismissed that with a gesture and said to the maid, "Put the tray there, Yolanda."

He pointed toward the dark coffee table. There was none of the softening of a 'please' that Mama or Papa would have added.

The maid nonetheless smiled with straight teeth that sparkled as white as her apron. "Sí, Señor."

She steadied the pitcher and leaned over to set the silver tray on the tabletop.

The white cotton of the dress and apron tightened against her breasts and stomach, and suddenly it was as if I were looking again at Old Dicey's young niece back in their New Orleans shack. And I knew that Yolanda's plumpness wasn't due to pre-adolescent fat after all.

She was pregnant.

3

*W*HEN THE MAID straightened and made her servant curtsy in the direction of my grandfather, my pupils had adjusted so well in the dim room that I could distinguish her dimpled chin, straight nose, and high forehead below that abundant black hair and little white cap.

She tripped across the parlor carpet to the dining room arch and curtsied again to my grandfather before she slipped through the swinging door.

My grandmother poured liquid from the pitcher into a crystal tumbler and held it out. "Mr. Harrison." Her voice had reverted to the childlike lisp.

He took the glass with a brief nod, and I wondered if anyone in the household ever said 'please' or 'thank you.'

"Do you know anything about the war tensions?" My grandfather said abruptly, peering across the darkness at me. "Did all this current uneasiness make the news in backwater New Orleans where you've been living?"

He thought New Orleans was backwater?

But I merely nodded. "I've been following the declarations of war."

I didn't say I'd also been going to the Unique Theatre on Canal Street to see the newsreels—which showed hoards of men in uniform marching like inebriated ants through London and Paris streets on their way to war. "France and England and Russia have declared war on Germany and Austria. Turkey is planning to come in on the side of Germany, and Japan will probably decide to join England and France, but no one really knows if—"

My grandfather broke in with, "I didn't mean those war tensions!"

As my grandmother handed me a crystal tumbler, he shrugged impatiently. "No one believes there will actually be a war in Europe. The European declarations are all posturing and speechmaking. It's all politics aimed at the 1914 elections. I meant the war that may break out any moment here on the border."

"Oh."

I took a swallow of the lemonade, wishing it had been plain water.

"Trouble here has been simmering between the revolutionaries since Madero was assassinated last year." For the first time he sounded impassioned. "Carranza and Villa are bickering among themselves now, and the conflict could spill over the border any time and drag El Paso into it. President Wilson has sent Scott and Pershing to Fort Bliss to keep a lid on things. He doesn't want to fight a bunch of Mexican bandits."

"Oh," I said again.

I knew all about the European war, but I hadn't the slightest idea what border conflict he was talking about. Before I had to say something ignorant, however, my grandmother murmured, "This drink is actually limeade since everyone in Mexico picks limones green. I always insist on plenty of sugar. I hope it's sweet enough for you."

While I was trying to think of a diplomatic way to tell her it was too sweet, she mused on in that feigned little girl chirp, "Isn't 'Cooper' rather a strange name?"

I didn't say that 'Cooper' was no stranger than 'Davis.' I merely said, "It was my mother's family surname."

"Oh, yes." She swiveled her bird-thin neck, and the diamond pin, the diamond studs, twinkled despite the shadows. "This morning saw the last of the ice, Mr. Harrison. We need another block for the ice box if we're to have anything cool this week."

"I'll take care of it."

She may or may not have nodded as she busied herself passing out little hors d'oeuvre plates and napkins.

I saw that her rings were indeed encrusted with diamonds as I accepted a plate and napkin and put them in my lap.

Then she held out the footed plate of tiny sandwiches to my grandfather and said, "While you're downtown, Luther, do you think you should order from another bakery? I believe Mr. Lewis is foisting day-old bread on us for the price of fresh-baked loaves."

"Lewis is the only baker in town who slices his own bread, Angelica." He lifted off two little sandwiches. "You know you don't want to leave that to Yolanda."

"Of course not." She passed the plate to me.

I wanted to say 'thank you,' but she went on before I could. "Do feel free to eat as many as you like, Cooper. It will be a few hours until dinner, won't it, Mr. Harrison?"

He didn't answer and said to me, "I hope you like Mexican food. While we're between cooks, Yolanda has been pressed into service. But she only knows how to make ceviche and boil up a few stews."

I didn't know what ceviche was, and I contented myself with trying to decide what rules governed how my grandmother addressed him. I debated whether I should call him 'Mr. Harrison' or 'Luther' or perhaps 'Grandpa.'

And what was I supposed to call her?

I watched her put the serving plate down and select a sandwich. Then I picked up the vague outline of my sandwich and bit into it.

I hadn't thought I was hungry, but the crisp cucumber and the fresh white bread were delicious. I finished that canapé and ate three more while I drank my too-sweet limeade.

Then my grandmother, who barely sipped from her glass and

who hadn't taken a single bite of the sandwich, stood up. "Don't you think Cooper should go rest now, Mr. Harrison?"

She brushed imaginary crumbs from her taffeta skirt while my grandfather gave the tapestry bell pull a tug.

A few seconds later, the pregnant maid swept through the swinging door with its brief light, and my grandfather ordered— again without a 'please'—"Yolanda, show Cooper to her room."

"Sí, Señor." She curtseyed, crossed the parlor to a door nearly unnoticeable in the gloom. She opened it to an equally gloomy hallway. "This way, Señorita."

She waited for me to put down the plate and glass and feel for my gloves and Mama's purse.

"I'll send Yolanda up to wake you in time for dinner," my grandfather said.

"Thank you."

I was proud of myself that I'd managed to say it at least once before I followed Yolanda into the hall.

The carpet runner muffled the sound of our feet as we went up one dark flight of stairs and then another. The stairway creaked under us.

I held onto the banister and tried not to drop my gloves.

Everything had the murkiness of an institution, and I felt as if I were being led up the stairs of an asylum. I wondered if barred windows loomed behind the heavy drapes.

When we reached the second landing, the stairs ended, and Yolanda said, "Here we are, Señorita."

She opened a door, and sunlight gushed over us.

The sudden light was so bright that sun-spots danced across my retina. I shuttered my eyelids against the brilliance and realized I'd been holding my breath in the dark. I flattened my eyelids to protect my pupils while I walked into the room.

Two entire walls were windows hung with lace, and the room ached with sunlight.

The outline of a tall cottonwood loomed beyond the curtains, and I could hear dry leaves crackle in what must have been a breeze I couldn't feel.

Papa's trunk sat at the foot of a gleaming brass bed.

The bed was enveloped by a white bedspread and piles of white pillows. A white satin boudoir chair faced a mahogany dressing table covered by a white lace runner, and a milk-glass bowl of white silk flowers shared the runner with a milk-glass lamp.

I blinked hard against the bleached whiteness of everything.

Although I myself would have added a red cushion or a blue vase to relieve the white, whoever chose the furniture did have good taste, and I murmured, "This is a beautiful room."

"Sí. The furniture comes from Señor Harrison's store." She glanced around, obviously not interested in the room. "Do you want me to help you unpack now, Señorita?"

I put my gloves and Mama's purse on the white bedspread, and sat down on the bed. The brass jingled. "I don't need help unpacking, but I would like a bath."

She pointed and gave her servant curtsy. "The bathroom is in the hall."

I untied the ribbon from under my chin and started pulling Mama's hatpins from the black straw. But when I took off the hat and reached over to lay it beside the purse and gloves, Yolanda gasped.

She swooped and grabbed it. "It is bad luck to put a hat on a bed, Señorita!"

I watched her take Mama's hat to the bureau, and her superstitious fear made her seem very young. Which in turn made me feel quite friendly toward her, and I asked in a spirit of comradeship, "How old are you?"

"Dies-y-seis ." And in case I didn't understand, she translated, "Sixteen. I was born veinte, twenty, years to the day from the birth of General Francisco Villa. The general is thirty-six now. He and I share the same name day."

My grandfather had mentioned the name 'Villa' a few minutes

earlier, but since that didn't mean anything, I said, "I guess I don't know who General Francisco Villa is."

"You don't know who General Francisco Villa is!" Her disbelief echoed across the whiteness, and she retreated a step. "He is the greatest of all Mexican generals!"

I didn't confess that I didn't know the names of any Mexican generals.

She stared at me. "You must have seen General Francisco Villa in the newsreels!"

I couldn't admit my ignorance, so I murmured instead, "If you've seen newsreels, I guess you can go to the pictures."

"Of course I can go to the pictures." Sunlight reflected from the white lace runner, from her uniform and white cap.

I topped her by a few inches, but she held the advantage of being in her own surroundings and of being a year older, so I heard myself muttering lamely, "It's just that my grandfather thinks moving pictures are a waste of time and money. I guess old people can't adjust to new inventions like airplanes and motion pictures."

"Your grandfather is no more than fifty."

I envied the certainty in her voice, and I felt my face grow warm. "Well, I think fifty is old," I said.

"It is not old for men on the border, Señorita. A lot of men are not successful until that age."

I probably could have held my tongue if I hadn't been so hot and sticky, if I hadn't come across Texas to the end of the earth, where I didn't want to be. I might not have said anything if either of my grandparents had greeted me with enthusiasm. I might have even controlled myself if the room hadn't throbbed with such intense light. But as it was, I said, "And you found someone successful to marry?"

She stared at me a moment before she tossed her head. "No," she said as she flounced out the door.

4

$\mathcal{I}$ SAT ON THE WHITE bedspread and watched her white uniform blur down the stairs.

I knew I'd spoken out of turn.

What had come over me?

What had made me ask such a rude and pointed question?

I stared out the door into the dark hallway and let my shoulders sag.

I'd been in the house less than an hour and I'd already insulted my grandparents' maid. I'd ruined my chance to make a friend and had instead made an enemy.

An enemy of the one person I'd probably need more than anyone else.

She could have helped me improve my rudimentary Spanish, could have taught me about El Paso and Mexico. I particularly needed to figure out how to relate to my grandfather. And since she could have explained all those border troubles I hadn't a clue about, I'd also thrown away my chance to appear less stupid to him.

She also went to the pictures, and maybe she could have gone with me to the Bijou. If I hadn't been so rude.

I sighed.

Well, there wasn't anything I could do about my tactlessness now.

Mama had always cautioned me not to blurt out what couldn't be unsaid, but she'd added that once the words were spoken, there was no sense bemoaning them. "Don't even think about spooning up that spilled milk," she'd laugh.

I got off the bed, and the brass rails jangled off-key while I went to Papa's trunk and knelt down on the carpet.

I sighed again.

My one consolation was that at least I'd held my tongue long enough to board the train from New Orleans. I'd left for El Paso before I'd told Mama's friend Rosalie that her new husband appeared much too frequently whenever I stood on the back porch helping old Dicey scrub clothes in sudsy water. I hadn't mentioned that he offered to dry off my bare arms much too eagerly. And I didn't bring up his too frequent stares at me across the dinner table when Rosalie went to the kitchen for that other helping of dessert pudding or the extra cup of coffee he'd requested.

At least I'd let Keith Boudreaux hug me good-bye without shoving him away or mouthing something I couldn't take back.

I sighed again, unfastened the clasps of Papa's trunk, and opened the curved lid.

I needn't have worried about things being jumbled around since I'd packed everything so well that nothing moved during the journey.

I took out the two dresses on top and laid them, crushed and wrinkled, on the bed.

How could I bring myself to ask Yolanda to press them for me now?

I wouldn't blame Yolanda if she avoided me completely. My question had been not only rude, but downright unkind. I knew better than to pry.

And I certainly knew better than to pry with a question about whether a pregnant girl was to be an unwed mother or not.

I'd been on my own since Mama and Papa died, and I should have been more adult.

I unloaded the layer of books and stacked them on the carpet. They smelled of leather and ink.

Then I took out the copy of *Tarzan of the Apes* I'd shoved down beside my two extra pairs of shoes. I'd bought the book just before I left, and I'd been reading it on the train. When the train reached El Paso, I marked my place with a postcard Papa had sent from a church retreat before the flu epidemic hit.

I opened the book and read Papa's handwriting. *"I'll be home on Thursday. We'll go to the St. Louis for café au lait."*

A terrible sadness filled my chest, and I turned the card over quickly to look at the drawing of a dog with a handlebar moustache. He stood on his hind legs in a cowboy outfit and aimed a pair of six-guns with his front paws. Papa had sent the postcard because he knew the cartoon would make Mama laugh.

Mama had always laughed a lot.

I avoided looking at Papa's handwriting again as I slid the card between the pages and got off my knees to line the books on the bureau beside Mama's hat. Since I didn't have bookends, I put my fat copy of *Pride and Prejudice* on one end and Trollope's thick *Eustace Diamonds* on the other while I tucked my photo album into the row of fiction.

Then I finished unpacking, putting things in the bureau drawers and closet, and propping a teddy bear, a present Papa had brought when the bears first came out, on the satin pillows.

Even if they were all brown, the books and the bear and Papa's trunk gave some color to the white room.

I unlaced and took off my patent leather boots. Then I padded in my stocking feet into the hall to try each of the three other doors.

The first door revealed a storeroom jammed with furniture and boxes, the next was locked, but I opened the third to a large room with a tile floor and two stained glass windows done in shades of green. A porcelain toilet, a pedestal washbowl, a huge bathtub with four eagle-claw feet, and a water heater—which Papa had always called a 'boiler'—were positioned around the walls.

Pat
Carr
Sunlight beamed through the emerald glass and turned the bathtub green, but I knew it was white enamel, exactly the kind Papa had ordered for the New Orleans rectory, and I felt doubly sad as I looked down at it.

I inhaled a few breaths.

Then I went to the water heater and found a box of matches on the windowsill. I had to strike three matches to get the gas jet in the heater to light, but at last it caught, and I went back to the bedroom, picked up my dresses and two hangers, and carried them to the bathroom.

While I waited for the column of water to warm, I took the green towel off the rack and attached the hangers with my wrinkled dresses to the brass bar.

There was nothing more I could do, so I stood in the green haze and tried not to think.

Finally, I locked the bathroom door, undressed, and turned the water on full force.

If I drowned in the tub or got asphyxiated by the gas from the water heater, my strong, fifty-year-old grandfather could break down the door.

The bathtub was so deep that when I stepped into the hot water, I could lean back with my neck against the smooth enamel curve and submerge myself.

I gazed at the hanging dresses through the soothing jade light and let myself wonder why my grandparents had never come to New Orleans.

They were the only living relatives I had, but I'd never met them until that afternoon.

I'd seen right away that an uncomfortable tension existed between them, but that didn't explain why we hadn't ever seen each other before.

Even if it was 1208 miles, the trip from New Orleans to El Paso wasn't difficult, not with the kind of luxury travel my grandparents could afford. The Southern Pacific had rails all the way from Louisiana to California, and there were stops all along the route. I'd already concluded that my grandfather took care of everything, and, even if my grandmother did have to travel with a dozen steamer trunks, he could have arranged the journey at least once in the past fifteen years.

Mama and Papa had been only children, and I was an only child. And Papa had no aunts or uncles. All the relatives I'd ever heard about were my two sets of grandparents, and the Coopers were both dead.

Most of the kids at my school were Catholics, and they all had dozens of relatives. All of them had scores of brothers, sisters, and cousins show up for graduation, and I'd envied all the babble and the squealing of their congratulations. I'd had only Rosalie and Keith in the chairs reserved for me, and I certainly hadn't relished seeing Keith Boudreaux.

I veered my thoughts from that memory to consider my grandparents.

So what happened to keep them from visiting New Orleans?

Why hadn't they ever come to see their only son? Their only grandchild?

My grandfather traced his ancestry back to an English manor, so he must have been proud of that fact. But now it seemed as if the American branch of the Harrisons had been hacked off at the root.

The meager pictures in the photo album I'd brought took up only a few pages. Rosalie had given me a studio photograph of Mama wearing the strings of pearls she'd given her for her birthday. There were two photos of Mama's late mother, one of her dead father in his Confederate major's uniform, the photograph of Luther and Angelica Harrison in a touring car, and Mama's and Papa's wedding picture. I'd rescued those few along with a baby picture of myself before all the contagious things from the house had been incinerated.

Pat

Carr

Those were my mementos.

I had to face the fact that no one living on earth was any longer related to me except Luther and Angelica Harrison.

They were all the family I possessed.

And I was all the family they had.

Why hadn't they ever come to see us? Me?

I abruptly sat up in the water.

But even stranger was the fact that Mama and Papa had never brought me out to the desert to visit my grandparents.

What could have happened between Papa and his parents in those fifteen years since I was born?

5

OF COURSE, I HADN'T expected Mama and Papa to die. But why hadn't they told me anything before they'd packed me off to Memphis? I didn't even have a farewell note.

I lay back in the water and stayed until it cooled, then I washed my hair, soaped and rinsed the train grime off the rest of me.

While the bath water gurgled down the drain, I turned off the flame of the boiler and wrapped myself in the towel. I scooped up my wadded travel outfit to cross the hall.

In the harsh sunlight, I saw that the bath towel wasn't green but as white as the bathtub.

I redressed in fresh underthings and petticoat, and while I was dragging one of the still rumpled dresses over my head, a knock sounded on the bedroom door.

"Señorita. Dinner is served in the dining room."

"Thank you."

But it took a long time for me to comb the rats out of my too-curly hair, put on my stockings and a pair of indoor slippers. Then I paused to give the bear a hug, and by the time I opened the door to the landing, the hallway stood empty.

I hated to plunge back into that darkness, but there was nothing for it, and I clung to the banister as I went down the squeaking stairs.

I only hoped I'd be able to find the food on my plate in the gloom.

When I reached the parlor and opened the door, however, I saw that I wouldn't have to fumble for silverware since candles burned in the dining room chandelier.

The chandelier had holders for a dozen tapers, but only four were lit, and they cast a weak, wriggling light over the table and buffet. But even faint candlelight was better than the afternoon darkness, and I easily found the place set for me.

A great expanse of while tablecloth spread out in both directions. My grandmother, elevating her chin in the regal manner of a porcelain doll, nodded to me even as she gazed off into space, but my grandfather at the opposite end of the table watched me sink into my chair.

"The soup is gazpacho," he said as I picked up my soup spoon. "I thought cold soup would be good in the heat. And I told Yolanda to spare the jalapeños until you get comfortable with spicy food."

So my grandfather even planned the meals. Maybe my grandmother was too sickly to do anything.

Was she simply too frail to travel?

Or couldn't her pale eyes face daylight?

I couldn't very well ask her if she had a disease or something, so we all sat and ate the cold soup in silence.

When Yolanda brought in the ceviche—which turned out to be cubes of fish combined with chopped onions, tomatoes, and peppers—my grandfather began to talk about antiques.

I tried to pay attention, but my mind kept wandering. And since halfway through the fish concoction, I realized that he might as well have been lecturing in a hall, I glanced at him and nodded occasionally while I gave myself over to eating.

After the ceviche came a stew, then a salad with something my grandfather called a jícama. The dim candlelight made spearing the unfamiliar vegetable awkward, but I managed to finish everything on every successive plate until at last Yolanda brought in a flan, which was vanilla custard with caramel drizzles.

I ate that, too, and when Yolanda replaced the dessert dishes with cups of coffee, my grandfather said, "I'll be leaving on a buying trip to Mexico soon if war doesn't break out, so we have a lot to accomplish at the store."

"Why does everyone keep speculating about a border war?" my grandmother asked with a pout, and I concluded she slipped in and out of the little girl role whenever it suited her. "It's between the rebels and the government, and it has nothing to do with us."

My grandfather didn't answer, and I decided silence was one of his ways of keeping the upper hand.

I nearly sighed. Already I understood more than I wanted to.

While we drank the coffee laced with milk, I also began to get a little angry. Why hadn't either of them asked me anything about New Orleans?

On the train, I'd imagined they'd like to hear about their only son, and I'd planned to tell them how everyone in the church admired him, how—despite anxiety about the flu—people from all across the state came to his funeral.

But the meal was ending without either of them even bringing up Papa.

"I want to be at the store early tomorrow," my grandfather said as Yolanda came back for the coffee cups. "We'll have our tortillas and eggs at six."

"Sí, Señor."

"I don't get up that early, Cooper," my grandmother said.

And since that was as good an exit line as any, I rose from the table. "Good night," I said as levelly as I could while I went through the arch and felt for the hallway door around my exaggerated, dancing shadow.

By the time I made my way up to the bedroom, the dusk outside was as dark as the staircase. Twilight stained the horizon purple, and I lifted the curtain to see the mountain peaks flattened into two-dimensional cardboard cut-outs.

I liked them better as black construction paper hills, and I stood, purposely not thinking about my parents or my grandparents, feeling my irritation fade into sorrow while I watched the violet clouds darken and disappear.

But the sky didn't turn black. Instead it edged into a strange greenish midnight blue, hanging between the night colors until finally it became somber enough to reveal stars as big as tack heads. The constellations glittered vast and still, and I stood a few minutes, immersed in the sadness of it.

At last I dropped the curtain.

But I didn't click on the electric overhead. I could see well enough to undress, unload the pillows and the Roosevelt bear, and climb into the jingling brass bed.

6

$\mathcal{T}$HE NEXT THING I heard was a tap on the door. "Señorita. Breakfast is ready."

Sun already shone on the cottonwoods.

I hurried to dress, but my grandfather was crumpling his napkin beside his empty coffee cup by the time I made it to the dining room. No candles flared now, and the room had been re-entombed, but I could nonetheless distinguish a plate of eggs at my place.

"Don't you have an alarm clock?"

I shook my head and poked my fork into the yolks. They oozed over a hazy disk I decided must be a tortilla.

"Why didn't you say something? I'll get you one." He stood up. "I left the store closed all day yesterday. We need to get there early."

"I'm not hungry." I started to push back my chair.

"You will be by ten o'clock. Sit still and eat. Come out when you've finished."

I forked up everything on the plate without tasting it before I rushed out the front door into the morning sunlight. The day was strangely cool.

My grandfather, gloved, vested, and coated under the black slouch hat, waited behind the wheel of a black Model T Ford that was equipped with an enclosed wooden truck bed. It was the kind of ungainly, top-heavy conveyance Papa called a 'pie wagon,' and despite the fact that gold script on the wooden side proclaimed grandly HARRISON AND ROBARTS ANTIQUES, it was hardly elegant.

My grandfather watched me read the lettering and said sternly, "This is convenient for hauling antiques. Get in."

The motor was already running, so I grabbed the hand rail, climbed onto the running board, and slid into the passenger seat.

My grandfather snapped the top half of the windshield into place, released the brake, and worked the pedals.

We took off at once, putt-putting past the fountain, down the gravel drive, and out onto the dirt street. There was no traffic as we retraced the route from the day before, and soon we were back on the broad, paved street among the downtown brick buildings.

No cloud passed across the nearly white sky, and the day was already heating up.

Suddenly, shots rang out.

My grandfather swerved the truck onto the sidewalk and grabbed the hand brake to stop us just before we hit a streetlamp.

I was jolted into the windshield as the motor coughed and died.

My grandfather threw an arm across my back and dragged me to the wooden floor below the dashboard.

Another volley of bullets plowed into the yellow bricks above our heads.

"Stay down," my grandfather rasped.

As if I could move beneath the weight of his arm.

We lay wedged under the dashboard, and after what must have been five minutes, I decided I'd as soon be shot as suffocated.

But at last, when no more gunshots sounded, my grandfather lifted his arm and raised himself a few inches at a time. "I think it's clear," he whispered hoarsely.

There were no doors on the pie wagon to protect anybody in

the front seat, and I peered out at the street. "Why would anyone shoot at us?" I whispered back.

He felt for his hat, which had flown off when he'd jammed us onto the floor, and carefully eased around the steering wheel. He dropped to the sidewalk, crouched low, and said, "They were probably shooting at the truck."

"Who's 'they?'"

"Mexican bandits."

"Why would they shoot at your truck?"

"The soldiers from Fort Bliss drive Fords just like it to haul freight."

"Oh." I didn't ask why Mexican bandits would shoot at soldiers driving a pie wagon to Fort Bliss.

After another minute my grandfather said, "We'll walk the rest of the way. Scoot out this side. And keep your head down."

I did as he ordered.

There were no more shots, and the street remained empty except for the wind that came up as we inched along the side of the truck.

"I'll call the house and tell Tomás to come down later."

I brushed off my bodice. I needn't have bemoaned the wrinkles since now dirt streaked one sleeve and my skirt.

My grandfather didn't seem to notice as he grabbed my arm and guided me to the corner. "This is a block with cover," he said.

As he urged me along, my gaze caught the black ad on one yellow brick façade, THE ST. CHARLES IS A BULLET-PROOF HOTEL.

Why hadn't my grandfather told me things like that when he wrote the letter that approved my coming? How could I have guessed that the comic post-card dog with his six-shooter was no joke in El Paso?

I sheltered my eyes against the wind as we turned another corner. In a few minutes we passed the Bijou Theatre. Then my grandfather was unlocking the shop door and clicking on the lights. He snapped the lock again and left the CLOSED sign in place.

Fortunately, no one skimped on electricity in the store, and in the bright light I could see the furniture, the shelves, and the glass-topped counter across the back wall.

I'd even be able to see anyone who attacked the store.

My grandfather crossed the room and hung his hat on a brass hook while he tugged off his gloves, picked up the receiver from the wall phone, and whirled the crank.

"Give me 417," he said into the mouthpiece, and when after a few seconds Yolanda must have answered the phone, he added, "I want to speak to Tomás."

After another pause, he said, "Tomás, wait an hour and then get the truck. I left it on San Antonio Street."

I couldn't avoid hearing his half of the conversation while he explained what had happened and gave instructions to Tomás, and then to Yolanda, and finally to my grandmother.

"Angelica, don't send Yolanda out this morning. We were shot at on the way to the store." He listened and nodded even though she couldn't see him. "Of course, I'll call him. And I'll telegraph Mrs. Robarts. It could be war."

I looked around the store while he gave his commands.

The furniture had been dusted and polished, and someone— probably my grandfather since he handled every detail—had decorated the tabletops with porcelain figurines.

Two tapestry wing chairs sat on the display dais behind the plate glass window. Beside them was a low table holding an elaborate silver tea service.

I thought the window arrangement pretty vulnerable to stray bullets and found myself wondering who bought antiques in Wild-West El Paso anyway. Who would want to shop in a place where bandits fired at passers-by whenever they felt like it? My grandfather might as well ship everything to Samuel Robarts' widow in Philadelphia and be done with it.

When I glanced back at him, he was pressing the little stirrup of the phone and twirling the handle again. "Give me Fort Bliss. General Pershing's office." He gave another nod that nobody could see. "All right. This is Luther Harrison. Tell the general I was shot at this morning."

This time while he hung up he said over his shoulder, "General Pershing will be coming in." And then he surprised me by actually looking at me. "Did the shots frighten you?"

"No."

They'd been too unexpected to scare me, and I thought that maybe people have to anticipate something to panic.

But while I debated about adding that, he tucked at his vest, straightened the gold chain that hung across his broad chest from pocket to pocket and said abruptly, "All right, now tell me what you know about antiques."

What kind of an order was that to follow his concern about getting shot at?

I stood there looking at him.

"Well, do you know anything about antiques?" he demanded.

How much should I know to qualify as 'anything?'

"I know they're old," I said.

I couldn't tell if a brief smile or frown crossed his features as he turned away and went down an aisle between groups of furniture. He gestured at me to follow him.

"A bench or a stand must be at least seventy-five years old to be an antique." He stopped and put a hand on the spindle of a four-poster bed. "See this? It comes from the time of George Washington. Some pioneer family carried it across the plains in a covered wagon."

He watched me a second before he asked with the same abruptness, "Can you distinguish how this bed differs from that bed over there?"

The bed across the aisle had a six-foot, yellow headboard in solid wood.

He moved to it. "This wood with the dark grain is called 'tiger oak.'"

"Because it has the gold and black coloring of a tiger," I said.

My brain had begun to function, and I could listen readily to his explanations. Perhaps it wasn't such a bad thing after all to be fired upon first thing in the morning.

"But how do you know either bed is an antique?" I said. "How can you be sure that one was brought across Texas in a covered wagon?"

My grandfather gave me a long look, but I didn't flinch.

I merely gazed straight at him and added, "How do you know both beds weren't made yesterday?"

An expression of approval, so fleeting that I almost missed it, crossed his face. "Sometimes you can tell an antique by the style. But a lot of companies make good reproductions now, so you have to authenticate a piece with other clues."

I nodded.

"Here. Look at this ladder-back." He stroked the slatted back of the chair. "The wood is oak. Probably an original honey color. But the seventeenth-century varnish turned it into what looks like dark walnut."

I tabulated quickly. "That chair was made in the 1600s?"

"The first glance fools people. But once you recognize the varnish, you know the piece is at least two hundred years old."

I filed that information away.

We spent another hour walking through the shop, and he became so preoccupied that I was certain he'd forgotten all about being shot at.

I was also sure he didn't notice the cars beginning to chug down the street or the few shopkeepers and clerks scurrying by, leaning against the wind.

The plate glass in the window rattled, but my grandfather merely talked over the gusts. Since I didn't want to interrupt him, I followed him around the showroom, listened, and tried to soak up everything he said.

I was thoroughly enjoying myself and beginning to identify some characteristics of antiques by the time he finally paused to ask, "Do you have any questions?"

I had about twenty, but I asked the first one that popped into my head. "If you're gone, how do I know what to charge if someone comes in to buy something?"

I hadn't meant to sound so dubious about someone actually coming in to buy anything, but he didn't seem to notice as he splayed his hand toward the glass-topped counter. "The prices are in a book."

I nodded again. Then I said, "I like the way you display walnut bureaus with walnut tables, but what if a customer comes in and insists on buying that mahogany piano stool and that oak stand?"

"We can't demand that customers have taste. No matter how much we'd prefer to sell only to people who have it."

Since he seemed in a pleasant mood for the first time, I said quickly before I had to demonstrate my ignorance about something, "What do you want me to call you?"

He looked blank as if he hadn't thought of my calling him anything. "What do you call your other grandparents?"

"I don't have any other grandparents. Mama's parents died before she married Papa."

"I see." He tugged fingers through his hair and a few seconds went by. "I suppose 'Luther' will be all right."

"And will 'Angelica' be all right, too?"

He obviously hadn't thought of my calling my grandmother anything either. "I suppose," he said.

He looked out the front window, seemed to notice the town coming to life, and motioned me toward the counter.

He unlatched the padlock and swept an unopened copy of The El Paso Times onto a stool. He raised the glass lid of the case and took out a leather book with CASH embossed in gold across the cover.

He put it under his arm while he reached in and lifted out a bracelet of dark red polished stones. "I keep the semi-precious jewelry in here. People are able to afford these pieces." He grimaced again and added, "And some females pretend they'd rather wear semi-precious stones than diamonds."

He angled the bracelet back and forth, and under the electric light, wine-colored sparks flashed. "This is a good set of garnets."

Just then someone rapped loudly on the front door.

A man was peering through the glass and wobbling the doorknob noisily. "Luther! If you're going to have the lights blazing, you may as well take down the sign that says you're closed!"

I could see a khaki jacket intersected by a black belt and a black diagonal strap. The black bill of a khaki cap pressed against the glass in the door. Fortunately, the soldier held a riding stick rather than a pistol in his gloved hand.

He pushed the cap back from his forehead and tried the knob again before he re-applied the butt of the crop to the door. "Luther! Open up!"

My grandfather—Luther—replaced the garnet bracelet and lowered the glass lid.

He put down the ledger and padlock and walked across the room with a stride that seemed too heavy for such a short man.

I stayed behind the counter as he unlocked the door.

When the soldier bent to come inside and straightened to at least six feet, I could tell that his uniform belonged to an officer.

He towered very tall and very thin over my grandfather as he tugged down the flaps of his jacket and took off his billed cap.

He ran his palm across his close-cropped hair, and smoothed the rectangle of his gray-speckled blond mustache. "Just as I was leaving, Captain Murray told me you called. He said you were shot at this morning."

Luther craned his neck to look him in the face. "Has the war started, Jack?"

"I'm afraid so. I got a wire this morning. The French attacked the Germans on the frontier yesterday."

7

"I DIDN'T MEAN THE European war. I meant the hostilities on the border. Did the shots this morning indicate Mexican revolutionaries are firing at Americans? Have they started a war?"

"Of course not." The officer pulled off his gloves. "They may not like us and they may not trust us as far as they can throw us, but all the revolutionary parties and all the loyalists are vying for America's approval. Nobody on the border is the kind of fool who wants a war with us."

"The shots were too close for comfort."

"You know that if those remnants from what's left of the federal army or Villa's bunch of brigands chase each other anywhere near the river, the bullets reach Stanton Street. You know that's why Scott and I are insisting on an arms embargo." He moved to the counter, and I guessed that if he hadn't already taken off his cap, he would have when he saw me. His eyes sparkled and he re-smoothed his graying blond hair while he smiled. "I didn't know you had a new assistant, Luther."

"My granddaughter Dav—Cooper. This is General Jack Pershing."

"I didn't know you had a granddaughter either." He reached across the counter. "What a fascinating name."

I took his outstretched hand, relieved for a change that I could shake hands with someone who had fingers larger than mine.

"Cooper arrived yesterday," Luther said. "From New Orleans."

I was doubly relieved that he didn't make a big production out of my name this time.

"You remind me of my oldest daughter. My Helen has that same intelligent, straightforward look." The general studied me with blue-gray eyes. "Were you worried that a war had started on the border the day after you got here?"

I shook my head, and because he gazed at me with such understanding, I let myself say, "I guess I don't know enough about the border yet to be worried."

His smile broadened, and I took a breath.

"But has war really started in Europe?" I debated calling him 'Sir,' but I let it go. "When I left New Orleans, people were still hoping there wouldn't be any actual battles."

"The French and Germans couldn't wait to start an actual battle." The bristles of his moustache twitched. "Both countries want to control Alsace-Lorraine. They were determined to fight no matter what anyone else did."

He spoke as if I'd know what he was talking about. "I told your grandfather war was inevitable. Everyone wants more land and more respect. The generals are also testing out the new weapons they've stockpiled all over Europe."

"Well, that bandit Villa keeps talking about how he wants respect. He threatens to confiscate land from foreigners and pass it out to the peasants. And now he's bought a dozen bi-planes. Of course he'll need to test them by flying over El Paso. Where does that put the odds for a border war?"

General Pershing gave an indulgent chuckle. "Don't exaggerate, Luther. Villa hasn't touched a single American-owned hacienda, and he bought five bi-planes. But everybody knows he doesn't have a man in his so-called army who can fly a plane. We all know he's more interested in outfitting his special train with a parlor car and flush toilet than he is in finding a pilot among his rag-tag followers."

Luther shrugged good-naturedly. "If you say so, Jack." Then he turned to me. "General Pershing and I are going over to the Hotel Del Norte for coffee. Do you think you can keep the store while I'm gone?"

I couldn't imagine a stampede of customers crowding through the door, and I nodded.

"All right then." He came around the counter, got his hat, and patted the ledger. "The prices are in here. If you don't recognize a piece by name, just tell the customer to wait for me." He pulled the gold chain from his vest pocket and extracted a gold watch. "If someone comes and asks for a special item, tell him I'll be back in half an hour."

I nodded again.

"Good-bye, Cooper," the general said. "It was a pleasure to meet you."

I watched them go out and slant into the wind as they ducked under the flapping awning.

Beyond the buildings across the street and the dirt-brown hills that pressed too close to the buildings for comfort, the sky spread out, pale Wedgwood blue.

By the end of the day before, I knew that my grandfather controlled everyone around him, one way or another, and that he made all the decisions about the house and business. But I'd also decided by the time I'd stretched out in the brass bed that I wouldn't let him make all the decisions for me. I'd do my best to avoid arguing with him while I educated myself about antiques. But I wouldn't knuckle under to his rules.

I returned the newspaper to the counter, dragged the stool closer and half perched on it to lean into the case.

I'd resisted telling Luther that Mama and I honestly preferred jewelry with semi-precious stones. Mama always insisted the one thing she didn't need to keep track of was a diamond ring. "Plain gold will do just fine, thank you," she'd said and laughed.

I stared down at the handsome necklaces and bracelets in the case that sparkled with greater fire than the pallid rings and brooch my grandmother—Angelica—wore. She probably wouldn't have been any more vibrant draped in garnets, and since no jewelry in that house could be more than barely visible anyway, I supposed it was no great loss that she'd chosen colorless diamonds.

But why did she want to live in the dark like a bat?

A garnet ring glittered from a velvet ring box next to the garnet bracelet. The fiery red facets of the pieces matched, and I knew Mama would have liked the set.

I unfastened the loop and tongue of the lock to raise the lid and reach inside. I wriggled my finger into the ring and lifted it from the velvet box.

"Hello? Is the shop open yet?"

I nearly dropped the counter lid on my hand, and my head jerked up.

Two men stood in the center of the room.

Blood thumped into my temples. I'd been too engrossed to hear them come in.

How could I have missed the door opening and closing? Or the rush of wind?

I slipped the ring back into its velvet slot and let the glass top down slowly. The metal latch clicked together while I looked up at the two men.

The man in front wore a wide-brimmed Mexican sombrero, a tight black bolero over a white ruffled shirt, and tight black pants with silver buttons down each trouser-leg. A holster slung low on his hip revealed the silver handle of a pistol.

Had Mexican bandits stormed across the river under the cover of that morning's gun-fire? Had these two men crept into my grandfather's store to plunder his safe?

Then I saw that the second man, the one standing behind the Mexican hat, was older and wore the same kind of ankle-high laced shoes my grandfather wore. He had on a charcoal gray suit with vest, a celluloid collared shirt exactly like Luther's, and he sported a businessman's gray fedora and gray moustache. He also sucked on a toothpick.

He couldn't be a Mexican bandit.

"Is the s-shop open?" the first man repeated from under the cream-colored sombrero. His cleft chin was clean-shaven and he didn't have a mustache.

But he did have a faint stammer and the trace of a Spanish accent.

"We can come back later if you h-haven't opened the store yet."

I took a breath. "No, that's okay. The store's open."

He took off the wide-brimmed hat to reveal black hair and extremely dark eyes.

"I noticed a silver tea canister as we walked by the window." He pointed to the elaborate silver tea set—which I hadn't realized included a tea canister. "I've been looking for one like that for my m-mother."

Without his hat, he did seem young enough to be buying a present for his mother, and I wondered if he'd started to shave yet.

He lowered the hat to his side. "H-how much is the canister?"

I set aside the padlock and opened the leather cover of the ledger just as I realized I hadn't asked Luther if he'd alphabetized the items in the shop.

He hadn't.

After a couple of futile pages of Luther's spidery writing, I looked up at the young man and said—hoping the canister wasn't the centerpiece of the tea set, and hoping I hadn't given myself away with my hesitation—"It's twenty-five dollars."

"Isn't that a bit h-high?"

"It's sterling," I said.

I hoped it was.

"And it belonged to European royalty," I added quickly.

Technically it belonged to Luther, and surely descendants of minor English lords could claim some royal blood.

"Take it, Ed," the older man said around his toothpick. "You can afford it."

"Well, I thought—"

"Big movie star like you don't need to haggle."

Movie star?

The younger man blushed. "I guess people don't b-bargain on this side of the border, do they?" he said to me.

I didn't know, but I gave him a glance that could pass for either an affirmative or a negative as I edged around them to get to the window.

I reached for the silver piece and debated if I should alibi my soiled dress with the morning's shooting. But if they hadn't noticed the dirt, there was no use pointing it out. And there was certainly no use making them skittish by mentioning that people could get shot in El Paso. So I picked up the silver tea canister.

At least it felt light enough to be sterling.

As I carried it back across the room and went by the young man again, he stammered, "I'm Eduardo Jimenez. And this is Matt Gordon."

The fact that he introduced himself—with a Spanish accent and a stammer—would have made my own silence brusque and unfriendly, so I said as I angled behind the counter, "I'm Cooper Harrison. This is my grandfather's shop."

Eduardo Jimenez smiled and a dimple appeared in each cheek. "Matt and I just got into t-town. We checked into the Orndorff Hotel. Do you know if it's any good?"

I didn't say that I, too, just got into town and that I had no idea whether the Orndorff Hotel was any good or not. I didn't even know if it was bulletproof.

But since I remembered passing it, I side-stepped with, "It does have a nice view of the plaza."

"And you can see the alligators in the pool from our window."

Alligators in a pool in El Paso's downtown plaza?

I hadn't seen any such thing the day before when we'd driven past the plaza, and I didn't know if he was teasing, so I pretended to be too busy for a response.

Naturally, I hadn't asked Luther where he kept the wrapping paper, so I took up the front page of the newspaper—as if I always used newsprint to wrap purchases—while I stole a glance at the young man.

His outfit, with its silver buttons down the pants legs and his silver-handled pistol, did look like an elaborate theatre costume—in fact a rather silly one to be wearing in public so early in the morning—but I couldn't say that, so over the crinkling newsprint, I asked, "Are you really a movie star?"

"Well—" His blush surged back darker red.

"We come from Hollywood to meet General Villa. Ed's playing young Villa in the motion picture we're making of Francisco Villa's life," the older man said.

"It should be a good picture even if it does have me in it," the young man said with charming humility. He came to the counter and took a money clip from the bolero pocket. "You did say twenty-five dollars?"

I swallowed while I nodded. Was the price too high or too low?

To fill the awkwardness of my discomfort, I said, "You're actually making a motion picture of General Villa's life?"

"That's why we're h-here. Pancho Villa has invited us to meet him at his headquarters in Chihuahua. It'll be a great adventure."

"Some adventure," the older man muttered.

I was dying to ask if he knew the great actors like Mary Pickford or Charlie Chaplin. I didn't want to sound like a starstruck provincial, however, especially if the pose was a joke, so I kept my mouth shut.

"Villa's contract with the studio says he'll stage a battle in daylight so M-matt can catch it on film. Matt's the best cameraman in Hollywood."

He smiled so earnestly that I had to say something, so I blurted the first thing I thought of, "My grandfather calls Villa a bandit."

"He used to be," the young man agreed, smiling, not a bit defensive about someone he might be going to impersonate on screen. "But that's why he's so interesting. He's been—and done—everything. P-people see him as a romantic hero." He put a twenty dollar bill and a five on the counter with long slender fingers. "I hear he's very p-popular here."

I didn't know if General Villa was popular with anyone but my grandparents' maid, and I said, hoping it was true, "He's been in the newsreels a lot."

Then I handed the bundle across the counter to Eduardo Jimenez. "I hope your mother likes this."

His dark eyes crinkled in another smile. "She will like it very much, Cooper Harrison."

8

$\mathcal{I}$ STILL STOOD BEHIND the counter when Luther returned without General Pershing. He strode in, anchoring his hat and holding a fresh newspaper under his arm.

I said at once, "Someone came in and bought that silver tea canister from the window display. I couldn't find it in the ledger, so I sold it for twenty-five dollars. I hope that was all right."

"Twenty-five dollars!"

I handed him the bills.

"Twenty-five dollars!" he repeated.

His shock made me nervous.

Maybe the canister had been the centerpiece of the tea set.

"Was that all right?"

"All right!" He stuffed the money in one of the vest pockets, took off his hat, and in the same gesture ruffled the gray hair around his sun-burnt face. "That piece was worth at most two or three dollars."

"Oh."

"Who bought it?"

"A young man who was walking by. He wanted it as a present for his mother."

"Twenty-five dollars!" he murmured once more.

"I wouldn't want to cheat anyone. I told him it was sterling," I said crisply to keep him from marveling again. "So if it isn't—"

"It's sterling," he interrupted. "I don't carry plate. The silver wash wears off and all you have is discolored copper. If the man—whoever he was—asked for sterling, you sold him sterling."

"His name is Eduardo Jimenez. He told me he's a movie star from Hollywood."

Luther burst out with, "What nonsense!" and I knew I should have been more careful.

Knowing how he felt about the pictures, I was a ninny to bring them up, but since I'd already made that blunder, I added quickly, "He's in town with a cameraman. They're staying at the Orndorff Hotel."

"Well, since the wealthy Hollywood actor didn't balk at twenty-five dollars for a tea canister, there's no need for you to stop by the Orndorff to return any money."

His sarcastic tone indicated he didn't believe a word the young man had told me, and even though I wasn't thoroughly convinced myself that Eduardo Jimenez hadn't been joking about the movies or the alligators, I felt compelled to defend both him and my own gullibility, and I said, "They're going across the border to meet General Villa and film the story of his life."

"What nonsense!" Luther repeated.

But while he crossed the room, he gave a thoughtful hum.

And a few seconds later as he hung up his hat, he murmured, "In case you're right, I suppose I shouldn't take any chances. I'd better leave for Mexico immediately. If there actually are motion picture people crossing the border to film Villa, I can see them wandering around in the Mexican desert, getting lost or being captured by bandits and causing some international incident." He glanced at me. "As if the border needs more amateurs being kidnapped. Pershing has already issued orders that no outrageous ransoms are to be paid for anyone."

He pulled his fingers through his hair again. "Wasting time and money to make a film of Villa is just what some fool from Hollywood would think of."

I still felt defensive about the Hollywood people—and

myself—so I raised my chin and said, "I think a motion picture about General Villa would be interesting. The film people called him a popular romantic hero."

"There's nothing romantic or heroic about him. He became a general by getting rid of everyone in his way. He's the worst kind of bandit, as ignorant and pig-headed as they come."

Since only an hour earlier I'd determined I wouldn't argue with him—and since I'd already used up everything I knew about General Villa and Eduardo Jimenez—I didn't extend my defense.

In the silence Luther penciled an entry in his ledger while he said, "I suppose leaving first thing in the morning is my best option."

Then he opened a door and disappeared into the back room.

He didn't order me to accompany him, but when he didn't return, I followed him into what was obviously a storeroom.

Dust-festooned chairs straddled marble slabs, grimy crystal bowls sat on unpolished buffets, and scores of overstuffed burlap bags had been stacked against the wall. MAIZ had been stenciled in black across the burlap.

Luther stood sorting through a stack of red and blue blankets.

"If you are right, and I have to contend with blundering amateurs when we get to Villa's headquarters—" He let the possibility hang in the air.

"You and Tomás are going to General Villa's headquarters?"

He selected a pair of blankets and didn't glance at me. "Except for pockets of federal soldiers left behind by Huerta when he fled the country, Villa controls the Chihuahua countryside." He swung his arm toward the sacks. "I trade corn for anything of value his foot soldiers have to barter."

So he bartered food for antiques.

I frowned. "I thought you didn't like General Villa."

"Like or dislike has no place in business."

I couldn't stop myself. "But you just said he's the worst kind of bandit."

"Banditry isn't an issue either." He glowered. "Of course Villa's a bandit. His peasant 'revolutionaries' gun civilians down in the street and systematically loot the haciendas belonging to Mexican landowners or to the Spaniards and the Chinese. Villa hates all three with an equal passion, so his lawless gangs, his so-called 'soldiers,' have a license to kill and a license to sell anything they 'liberate' from the wealthy."

"But that means you're buying stolen goods?"

He gave me a sharp look. "I gather that would have bothered Alex."

It was the first time anyone had used Papa's name, and I felt my throat tighten as I stared into Luther's gray eyes. "Papa always said that the worst things you could do were to wound people deliberately and to steal the things they needed in order to survive."

"That high moral system may have worked for Alex in a parish church. But it doesn't work on the border. Mexican peasants wound and kill each other for the sheer sport of it, and they need everything in order to survive."

I knew I shouldn't keep it up, but I nonetheless said, "Papa always insisted that if people value something, they deserve to keep it."

"Alex was always an innocent," he said grimly. "These lawless peasants don't even know what they value. Thievery is such a way of life that they don't care what they steal or sell. If a merchant refuses to buy an antique, these rebels simply chop it up for kindling. They tore pages from priceless fifteenth-century incunabula to use as butcher paper." He put the remaining blankets back on the shelf. "The treasures from the haciendas were stolen long before I see them. It's not as if I'm a party to the looting. It's not as if I'm encouraging it."

Papa could probably have thought of something to contradict that rationale, but at the moment I couldn't come up with anything, so I was relieved when a knock sounded on the storeroom door, and Luther strode over to unlock it.

Tomás stood in the bright sunlight holding Raphael's reins.
"Señor Harrison, I have come with the wagon. Whoa, Raphael.
Yolanda will bring the lunch at noon."

I took a breath of sunshine as I edged past Tomás and stepped outside. Contradicting Luther had given me a headache.

Raphael turned a great brown eye toward me, and I went up to him to stroke his mottled nose.

"Whoa, Raphael," Tomás cautioned again even though the horse hadn't moved anything but his head.

Luther handed Tomás the blankets, then pulled the gold pocket watch from his pocket again and scowled at it. "All right, Tomás. Get started loading. We're leaving for Mexico tomorrow."

"Mañana?"

"That's what I said."

"Sí, Señor Harrison." Tomás tugged his hat brim toward me. "Buenos días, Señorita Cooper."

Before I could murmur a greeting, Luther broke in with, "Remember the corn is in fifty-pound sacks. So divide the weight evenly in the wagon."

"Sí, Señor Harrison."

Luther pocketed the watch and said to me, "Leave the horse alone. You can spoil a work animal with coddling. Come inside. I want you to polish a silver punch bowl I sold last week."

The least I could do would be not to argue about showing affection to animals, so I gave Raphael's nose one more pat and followed Luther.

When I came in, he was dragging a huge footed punch bowl from a cupboard. Festoons of silver fruit and leaves wove in bas-relief around the silver rim. Tarnish had darkened the large bowl into a rainbow of colors, and the plums in the elaborate decoration had turned a gleaming purple.

Luther gathered up some polishing rags and went into the showroom to set everything on the counter. "You do know how to shine silver, don't you?"

"Yes." I selected a buffing cloth.

Luther watched me a second, but finally he took the newspaper off the counter and went to the seventeenth-century ladder-backed chair he liked so much. He sat down and glanced at me once more while he unfolded the front page.

I rubbed hard strokes across the expanse of tarnished silver curves and around the intricate bas-relief fruit.

Luther hadn't really believed that Eduardo Jimenez was a Hollywood actor, but just in case I was right, he was starting his buying trip sooner than he'd expected to.

What he called a 'buying trip' anyway.

He considered General Villa and his men bandits, but he nonetheless traded with them and accepted their stolen goods. And no matter how he might try to explain away his tactics, he took advantage of them by exchanging cheap corn for precious antiques.

Just whom would Papa consider a bandit under these circumstances?

Luther rattled the paper, turned and folded another page while I polished a silver apple and surreptitiously studied his ruddy face.

He had broad shoulders and a broad chest, and he must have been twice as strong as Tomás, but he left the lifting and loading to his spindly-legged little driver. That, too, was probably part of being a businessman on the border. A wealthy employer couldn't coddle his workers any more than he could spoil his dray horses, so he had to let his hired help do the physical work. Yet at the same time—

He looked up just as I slid another glance at him.

He frowned. "I don't want Tomás to take all day getting those sacks on the wagon. Go check on how the loading is coming."

Of course he didn't say 'please.'

I dropped the polishing cloth in the bowl and went through the storeroom door to see Tomás in the sunlight outside, staggering up a makeshift ramp to the wagon bed.

He carried a bag of the shelled maize across his shoulders, and the planks of the ramp swayed under the weight. As he added the sack to the pile already in the bed, the springs whined, and the wagon shuddered.

Raphael flickered his ears and gazed back at Tomás and me. His folded-back ears seemed aggrieved.

Despite the fact that Tomás wore the brown hat, sweat poured down his forehead and streamed into his shirt collar. Widening patches of perspiration stained the front, back, and underarms of the shirt as he plodded down the ramp and ducked inside the hot shade of the storeroom.

I felt really sorry for him.

He was such a skinny little man.

He gave me his smile, and started to swing another bag off the stack.

I hurried over to him. "I can help put this one in the wagon."

"Oh, no, Señorita!" he cried in a shocked voice. "These bags—they are muy heavy."

He was right.

Fifty pounds of corn weighed more than I'd anticipated, and the sack was too bulky for me to catch the rough weave securely.

The burlap escaped from my fingers, and the bag slid off the pile before Tomás could grab it.

It thudded to the floor, a seam burst apart, and white and yellow kernels mounded into an instant hillock.

But along with the dried kernels, shiny cylinders with brass ends and conical tips tumbled out onto the wooden floor.

I watched dumbfounded as one of them rolled against my shoe and stopped.

No wonder the bags were so heavy.

Bullets had been buried in the corn.

9

MY THOUGHTS scattered in all directions. Luther was not only a fence but a smuggler!

I might eventually have made peace with the fact that he traded corn for priceless items looted from the great haciendas. As he said, he hadn't put the peasants up to stealing. And of course, since I understood that businesses had to show a profit, perhaps I could eventually have rationalized, just as Luther did, that the peasants couldn't do anything with the stolen goods except barter them away.

Naturally the hungry campesinos needed food more than they needed antique chairs or pages from fifteenth-century manuscripts, and even though Papa probably would have considered the transactions reprehensible, I might have finally accepted that Luther was just conducting business as usual on the border.

But smuggling bullets to a bandit in sacks of corn was something else again.

Papa would have had plenty to say about that.

Had Samuel Robarts known about the arms smuggling going on under his nose and under his name stenciled across the yellow bricks?

I glanced up as Luther's heavy footsteps came through the doorway and he demanded, "What happened?"

"It was my fault." I surprised myself with the steadiness of my voice. "I tried to help load a bag, and—"

"What were you thinking?" His steely eyes glared at Tomás. "You know a girl can't handle these bags."

I couldn't let Tomás take the blame, and I said, "He didn't ask for my help. I volunteered. But when I started to lift a bag, I couldn't hold it, and it slipped."

Luther scowled a moment longer. "Girls presuming to help," he muttered before he said to Tomás, "Get rid of all of this. And then go on with the loading."

"Sí, Señor Harrison."

"Come finish that punch bowl," Luther said to me as Tomás went out. "And don't volunteer for anything again."

He went back to the showroom as Tomás reappeared with a bucket, a tin dustpan, and a broom.

I wanted to console him, but I hadn't collected my scrambled thoughts enough to know what I should say, and Tomás began silently to sweep up the corn and bullets.

As the sweepings hit the metal sides of the pan, the bullets rang. As he emptied the dustpan into the bucket, bullets rang. But since Tomás didn't look up or acknowledge the sound of the metal against metal, I followed Luther in silence.

Papa wouldn't have kept silent.

And suddenly, I was pretty sure why Papa and Mama had never brought me to El Paso.

Papa had been the most principled man on earth. He couldn't abide dishonesty. And he must have found out somehow that his father was a crook.

Luther reached the ladder-backed chair as I came in.

He didn't sit down, however, but unfolded the newspaper and held out the front page. "I thought you might like to read the lead article in today's paper."

His voice had lost all sarcasm and gruffness, his tone had become mild, almost pleasant, and I wondered if he were trying to charm me into sanctioning his dishonesty.

Or perhaps he just wanted me to ignore the fact that his secret had spilled out onto the storeroom floor.

"One of his secrets at any rate," I thought grimly.

"It's an account of that first battle in the European war," he said. "The battle Jack Pershing mentioned this morning."

That morning his good friend Jack Pershing had also mentioned an arms embargo.

"It's a report that might interest you since you've been following the European war news."

From where I stood beside the half-polished punch bowl and the glass-topped case, I saw the bold black headline that took up a quarter of the page, FRENCH CAVALRY ATTACKS GERMAN POSITION.

Luther kept the paper extended until I forced myself to go around the counter and take the front page.

I stood there looking down at it and tried to focus.

But the European war had receded to a very distant place in my consciousness, and a minute must have gone by before the words quit jumping around.

It took me another few seconds to make the lines of print stay in their columns.

The war had interested me back in New Orleans.

I'd memorized the borders of Germany, France, Alsace-Lorraine, and I could have pin-pointed exactly where that initial battle took place.

But I no longer lived in New Orleans. And I could no longer concentrate on the European war.

Now I had too many other things on my mind.

I felt Luther's eyes studying me as I stood under the bright electric lights and scanned the page until the wriggling words began to make sense.

Just as General Pershing said, the war in Europe had indeed started.

The French and German armies had faced each other in a stand-off before the French cavalry had attacked a German unit, and had made "a brilliant and gallant charge into a hail of bullets from the German guns."

"Hail of bullets," loomed out at me.

I held the paper hard enough to wrinkle the edges, but the newsprint escaped again and merged into an image of bullets spilling, leaping, from the sack of corn in my grandfather's storeroom.

Probably the bullets fired at us that morning had been secreted in one of his bags of maize.

Of course, the people who'd fired at us that morning hadn't been firing at American soldiers from Fort Bliss. They'd been shooting at the gun-runner who carried ammunition across the border.

And Luther knew that.

"Jack Pershing is the only general in this country worth his salt," he was saying. His words blurred like the columns in the paper.

"He and General Scott have built Fort Bliss into the largest cavalry base in the country, but Jack's been insisting for months that using cavalry charges against machine guns only gets your men and your horses killed."

Jack Pershing insisted on an arms embargo, too.

Luther kept talking, but before I'd thought of a single thing to say, I glanced up at a movement in the shop window.

Yolanda walked past, lugging a huge picnic basket. She still had on the snowy uniform, but now instead of the little white cap, she wore a wide-brimmed straw sombrero, tied under her chin with a red ribbon.

Luther's voice stopped as soon as she opened the front door.

She closed the door, put the basket at her feet, and curtsied. "Are you ready for the lunch, Señor Harrison?"

He made an irritated gesture at her interruption and pointed to the table in the window display. "Clear off that tray and spread the food out there."

I thought it was a ridiculous place to eat lunch—and as vulnerable to bullets as it had been that morning—but Yolanda merely said, "Sí, Señor."

She bobbed again, carried the tea tray to a washstand, and set it down with a clatter. She untied her ribbon, took off the straw sombrero, and dropped it to the floor. Her black hair glistened under the electric lights, and I noticed that gold filigreed teardrops dangled from her earlobes.

As she went back to the window and began to unload the gigantic basket, Luther looked at me. "You can tell Tomás that Yolanda has come with the lunch."

I nearly mimicked, "Sí, Señor," but I conquered the impulse while I folded the front page of the newspaper and walked into the storeroom.

"Tomás, Yolanda has brought lunch."

"Bueno, Señorita." He'd nearly finished sweeping up the kernels of corn and bullets, but again he didn't look up or smile.

I went back to the main room and stopped beside the glass counter. I inhaled a couple of times and finally said as calmly as I could to Luther, "I didn't mean to keep this part of the paper."

"I finished with it," he said. "Yolanda, as soon as you unload all that food, carry a plate and a glass of coffee to Tomás in the storeroom."

"Sí, Señor Harrison."

She worked another few minutes, then took up a plate of sandwiches and a glass of milky brown liquid, and disappeared through the door to the storeroom.

I heard her murmur something to Tomás in Spanish, and I heard him answer in quiet Spanish.

Luther carried the ladder-backed chair to the window and put it up on the platform with the table and upholstered chairs. As he stepped onto the dais and sat down in the antique chair, he looked

at me. "Even though the café con leche is chilled, and these chick-
en sandwiches are meant to be served cold, there's no reason to let
the bread dry out." He took half a sandwich from a plate. "Come sit
down and eat."

It seemed stupid to exert my independence over a chicken
sandwich and a glass of cold coffee diluted with milk, so I laid the
newspaper aside and went to the window.

I felt like a fool climbing onto the dais and becoming part of
the display, but I nonetheless sat down in one of the tapestry chairs
as Yolanda returned.

I expected her to take the third plate and the third glass with
her into the storeroom to eat with her fellow servant.

But she didn't.

Instead she stepped up beside Luther and me and plopped
down boldly on the other tapestry chair.

Somehow the servant/employer relationship between Yolanda
and Luther had gone awry. It smacked of too much familiarity, and
now that I thought about it, her attitude held a strange undercur-
rent. Luther wasn't as much in charge as I'd thought.

And abruptly I knew why.

She was blackmailing him.

10

$\mathcal{A}$T DINNER THAT evening, I stirred my food around each successive plate, taking an occasional bite while Luther's conversation evolved into the same one-sided monologue as the night before. I knew more about antiques now and I wanted to listen, but too many things had happened, and I couldn't concentrate on what Luther said any more than I'd been able to concentrate on the European war news.

So I watched Yolanda as she brought in one course after another.

She had assured me grandly that she could do anything she wanted.

She could probably take anything she wanted as well, and I decided the gold earrings she'd worn to the shop had once been part of Luther's barter.

His shady dealings in Mexico certainly invited blackmail. And it would serve him right if he had to give up some of his loot to keep her quiet.

I wanted to get away from my grandparents, so as soon as the meal came to an end and Yolanda whisked away the coffee cups, I murmured "Good-night," and hurried into the hall.

I went up the stairs, and when I got to the third floor, I sat down on the dark landing.

I'd come to El Paso to get to know the only two relatives I had in the world.

In the thirty hours since I'd arrived, however, the only thing I'd gotten to know was that my grandparents weren't who—or what—I'd thought they were.

The afternoon before, even though I'd glimpsed hints of bitterness and pretense, I'd been secretly pleased to observe that my grandparents were rich. Papa had never earned more than a paltry salary from his collection plates, and Mama had had to budget carefully for everyday pillow ticking or winter boots. So the thought of living in comfort—actually in luxury—had seemed rather attractive.

Naturally, I didn't understand why my grandparents wanted to exist in a darkened velvet cocoon, but when I arrived, I'd nonetheless accepted their shadows along with their wealth, and I'd told myself I could put up with a little fakery.

But now I knew the darkness cloaked Luther's dishonesty as well as Angelica's artifice, and I knew the family wealth came from cheating Mexican peasants. Now I could no longer feel comfortable with the shadows or the opulence.

Nor did I know any longer quite how I felt about Luther himself.

I'd realized right away that he was bossy and imperious, that he treated his wife with sarcasm and disdain, but I knew I wouldn't allow him to treat me that way. That morning in the shop, I'd been impressed by his knowledge and love of antiques, and when I'd challenged him, I'd had the fleeting thought that he might even relish having someone around to match wits with him.

But then came the day's discoveries.

I tried to imagine what Papa would have said.

I folded my arms around my shins, rested my head on my kneecaps, and reminded myself that Papa hadn't a clue how commerce worked. I remembered him preaching sermons about rendering unto Caesar what was due, but I was never sure he approved of Caesar. He might have accepted that bartering for antiques was business, and he might have understood that if Luther didn't take the antiques, they could well be destroyed or bought by some other businessman. Perhaps a businessman who didn't even appreciate them.

But what about Luther's hiding bullets in bags of corn to supply a Mexican bandit? Would Papa have ever understood that?

During our early tour of the shop, Luther had explained about 'veneer,' a kind of fake furniture made by gluing thin layers of walnut or cherry to cheap pine so the furniture would look like the more expensive wood. I'd been reminded of Angelica, but I'd nonetheless assumed that Luther would never sell a veneer walnut desk as a solid wood piece, and I'd been pleased to compare his principles to Papa's.

But by noon, I recognized that Luther's stern appearance of being principled had also been just that—an appearance. I realized that 'veneer' described not only false night tables, but Luther himself.

I raised my chin from my knees and leaned my head against the banister.

Maybe I shouldn't have left New Orleans.

I'd have remained on familiar ground, and I'd have stayed ignorant about my grandparents, who would have kept in my mind the regal elegance they'd had in that Christmas photograph.

And I'd have stayed equally ignorant about everything on the border, which at the moment, sounded perfectly fine with me.

I stared morosely into the dark landing.

But then, what if I were jumping to conclusions simply because I was ignorant about El Paso and Mexico? I'd never heard of Francisco—Pancho—Villa before. I'd never even heard of the Mexican Revolution. But what if everyone along the border was caught up by the revolution in one way or another?

General Pershing certainly was.

Yolanda made no effort to disguise her involvement.

My grandmother might protest that the revolution had nothing to do with her, but since her pampered life in that diamond-studded cave came from Luther's dealings with the rebels, she'd actually become as involved as he was.

Even the motion picture people—if they were for real—planned to make a film of the famous rebel leader.

I sighed.

What if I were condemning Luther because I didn't understand enough? Pancho Villa obviously fought government forces. But was that a good thing? Was the government good or bad? Did rebelling against the government make Villa a hero or a villain? Which side was the right side?

Was Luther merely supplying a rebel for profit? Or was he doing a brave thing by helping an underdog?

How could I know what to think when no one was honest with me?

I sighed again and got up from the step.

The windows in the bedroom stood open, but now that the wind had died down, heat clamped like a lid over the room. I felt both stifled and ignorant as I changed to my nightgown and got into the brass bed.

The decorative polished brass knobs clinked, and brilliantly polished bullets rolled across my retina.

I dropped my head onto the pillow, certain I'd dream all night about those scattering bullets.

But the next thing I knew, a bird trilled outside my window, and I opened my eyes to daylight.

I'd forgotten all about asking Luther for a clock, and I sat up quickly and stared at the primrose pink sky. Surely it couldn't be later than six.

I threw off the sheet and hurried into a fresh petticoat and fresh stockings. I laced up my boots and rushed downstairs to reach the dining room just as Luther sat down at the table.

Flustered, I found my place in silence.

My fried eggs again mounded from congealing grease, but I ate them and the tortilla, and drank the steaming cup of café con leche Yolanda brought in.

"Pack sandwiches, some fruit, and some canteens of water, Yolanda. I want to reach Aguas de los Caballos by nightfall."

She murmured her usual, "Sí, Señor Harrison,"—as if getting to Aguas de los Caballos by nightfall happened every day—and went back to the kitchen.

I trailed after Luther to the front door.

We clambered into the pie wagon, and Tomás scurried from the back of the house to turn the starter crank. Since Papa had also driven a Model T Ford—although without the cabinet addition that made it good for hauling freight—I could have done the cranking myself, but I knew Luther would have been stunned if I volunteered, so I didn't.

Luther manipulated the choke and the foot pedals, and as soon as the motor hummed into a steady rhythm, he said to Tomás, "I'll drop these chairs for Mrs. Ames at the shop and leave the truck there, so bring the horse right away."

Tomás touched the brown hat brim. "Sí, Señor Harrison."

That morning, Luther and I reached the shop without getting shot at, and Luther drove past the Bijou Theatre to circle the block. He pulled the truck into the alleyway behind the store and braked beside the loaded wagon.

While he opened the back and took out two chairs, I jumped down from the running board.

He unlocked the door to the storeroom and glanced at me. "I intended to show you the safe this morning," he said. "But since I won't be gone more than a few days. I decided you don't need the combination."

I knew it was only his way of refusing to share authority, his way of holding tight to the reins, but I still felt heat flood my cheeks.

He must have noticed my flush, and he added, "Don't imagine that I'm questioning your honesty."

I couldn't suppress the thought, *"Questioning* my *honesty!"*

"It's just that if thieves rob a store, it's safer for a clerk to say truthfully that she doesn't know how to open the safe."

I couldn't help wondering what he had in the safe that he didn't want me to see.

"I'll be back in three or four days," he said.

The morning before, I'd been sorry he'd be going away just as I became acquainted with him, just as I realized how much I liked antiques, and I regretted I'd remain in a shrouded house with a shrouded grandmother while he journeyed to Mexico.

But this morning I wasn't the innocent I'd been the day before.

Now I didn't want to go with him. I didn't want to barter with poor people who had to give up their valuables if they wanted to eat, and I didn't want to be involved in the smuggling. Now I wasn't sure I'd feel anything but relief that he'd be gone.

So I merely stood beside the counter while he hung up his hat and got out the cashbook to explain his filing system.

His system didn't have any logical order that I could see, and I decided by the time he reached the end of the first page that I'd buy another ledger and alphabetize the merchandise for myself.

I nodded as he talked, however, until he finally closed the book.

Then he rummaged among the shelves to find a brass alarm clock. As he handed it to me he said, "This will go with the brass bed in your room. That bed came from Chapultepec Castle in Mexico City after Maximillian's defeat. It once belonged to the Empress Carlotta."

I didn't ask how many bags of corn laced with bullets the empress's brass bed had cost.

And since I succeeded in holding my tongue, he watched me a moment before he asked, "Is there anything you need to know before I leave?"

There was too much I needed to know.

But I nonetheless kept quiet again, and after another pause he pulled out the gold watch chain and removed a key. He put it on the counter. "This is to the front door. I told Yolanda to come scrub the floors today, so in the meantime, if you see anything that needs waxing, just tell her."

I tried not to gloat, but I couldn't help myself.

Her blackmailing made her as much a thief as he was, and it served her right to have to scrub floors and polish furniture.

Luther tapped the now-polished punch bowl. "Mrs. Hughes will come by for this sometime this week. She's throwing a party for General Scott on Saturday, so tell her I'll be back in time."

I nodded.

He made a circuit of the shop and delayed a moment beside the ladder-backed chair before he came to the counter and took some bills from his pocket. He held them out. "This should be enough for your lunches."

But I was too startled to reach for the roll, which I saw contained five and ten-dollar bills, and at last he laid the bills on the counter beside the front door key. "The Sheldon Hotel is expensive, and the dulceria down the street serves only candies. But I'm sure you can find some place to eat."

He went into the back room and unlocked the door to the alley.

He motioned to me and handed me that key as well. "You need to lock this after Tomás and I leave. You don't want someone pilfering from the storeroom while you're in the front of the shop."

Perhaps some hungry peasant stealing an antique chair to barter for food?

Luther opened the door, and I saw Tomás rounding the corner with Raphael and the picnic basket. His good humor had returned, and he acknowledged me with his toothy smile while he wedged the basket in beside the sacks of corn and blankets. He carried two canteens on lanyards slung around his neck and he laid them in the wagon before he backed Raphael into the wagon shafts.

Wind echoed down the alley.

Luther anchored his hat as he went outside and climbed onto the driver's box. Tomás fastened straps and harnesses, handed Luther the reins, and then lifted himself into the wagon. "Hasta la vista, Señorita Cooper."

Luther flicked the whip over Raphael's brown and white back. "I'll be back in three or four days," he repeated, and Tomás waved as they turned the corner.

And despite my cold disdain for my grandfather, an abrupt emptiness hollowed my chest.

11

I STOOD A MOMENT, staring into the wind and the harsh sunlight before I went inside and locked the storeroom door.

Then I walked through the shop, separated one of Luther's five-dollar bills from the roll, and crossed the street to Miller's Notions.

I was back in ten minutes with a new ledger.

I kept expecting Yolanda, but when she didn't appear, I let myself relax.

I didn't want to pretend to be her employer or tell her to wash any floors. Nor did I have any desire to find out how much money or jewelry she'd extorted from Luther.

So after a couple of hours, I gave in to my relief, told myself to think only about antiques, and set about organizing my ledger. I put a separate letter on each page and made sure I found the piece of furniture before I transferred names and descriptions from Luther's cashbook into mine.

Carved chair with red velvet cushion, early Spanish era, $15.

Chandelier, Colonial Mexico, $23.

Tea set, turn-of-the-century sterling, eight pieces, $55.

The canister was gone, and as I corrected the number of pieces to seven, I glanced up.

A little girl was sneaking into the shop.

Her dress hung too large from her bony shoulders, the ragged collar exposed her stalk of a neck, and the faded cotton hem dragged the floor. The leather on the toes of her shoes had scuffed away. She clutched the door handle as she crept in, as if ready to bolt.

"Can I help you?"

Her large brown eyes searched past me. "Ma told me to talk to Mr. Harrison. I got something to sell."

"Mr. Harrison won't be back for three or four days."

Her pale face crumpled.

"You can wait for him, or you can let me look at what you brought," I said gently.

She clung to the doorknob a moment longer.

Then her narrow shoulders quivered with determination and she stumbled to the counter.

The top of her head came to the rim of the glass cover as she reached in the sagging pocket of her dress to pull out a figurine. Her branch-like arm emerged from the sleeve, and her twig fingers put a blue porcelain dog on the counter. "Ma said Mr. Harrison likes glass animals."

I hadn't seen a glass animal anywhere, but I nonetheless picked up the dog.

ROYAL DOULTON had been baked in blue on the porcelain stomach, but the hind paw had been chipped.

"It belonged to Grandma," the little girl said. "Ma said Mr. Harrison might give a fifty-cent piece for it."

I didn't point out the chip. "I don't have a fifty-cent piece, but I have ninety-five cents in change."

Luther had given me lunch money, and it was mine to spend or not. "Would ninety-five cents be all right?"

She nodded solemnly.

I'd dropped the change from my purchase into an old Irish shaving mug, and I came around the counter with the mug. "Cup your hands."

I poured the coins into the grimy palms, and the thin fingers closed around them. "Don't lose any," I said, but before I finished saying it, the little girl scuttled away.

I watched her disappear, then I took up the blue cocker spaniel with its wavy porcelain ears and tail. It looked gaudy and sentimental and worthless, but I tucked it on a shelf beside a blue Wedgwood vase anyway. I could always chuck it in the trash with the ruined corn before Luther returned.

I went back to my alphabetical list and stayed busy until the red disk of sun hovered at the mountain peak behind Miller's Notions.

I relocked the front door and walked past the Bijou just as the electric bulbs blinked on and two girls about my age went inside, giggling and flirting with the boy selling tickets.

I tried not to envy them.

Despite the stinging sand flung by the wind, the way back to my grandparents' house wasn't nearly as far as it had seemed in the cart or the pie wagon, and I was passing the fountain before I'd quite prepared myself to sit with Angelica alone at the dining room table.

But since I couldn't stand around outside in the wind, I steeled myself to go in.

Angelica already waited at the table under the wan candlelight. As I sat down she murmured, "Mr. Harrison makes five or six buying trips a year, you know." A few seconds later, she said, "Mr. Robarts was never comfortable in the desert or with speaking Spanish. So he was content to let Mr. Harrison handle the Mexico end of the business."

I didn't ask if Mr. Robarts had been content to let Luther handle the smuggling as well, and we ate in uncomfortable silence until at last the café con leche arrived and I managed to tell Angelica that I'd had a long day.

"See Yolanda about breakfast," she said vaguely. "She's probably gone to the servants' quarters already."

I said I would later, but I decided that if two eggs and the slimy tortilla weren't at my place when I came down the next day, I'd skip breakfast.

In the morning, when I peered into the dining room, the dim plate with two cold eggs sat waiting, so I dutifully ate them. But before Yolanda appeared with coffee, I went outside and walked to the store.

I already knew the desert cooled down at night, and when I got to the shop, I luxuriated in the iced stillness until Yolanda came in carrying a little basket. She was wearing the straw hat and the gold filigree earrings.

She put the basket and hat down on a piecrust table beside a porcelain lady in a hoop skirt and went to the storeroom without glancing at me.

I worked on my ledger for a while until at last she came back into the showroom. "Did Señor Harrison want me to wash the front window?"

I didn't know, but I nodded anyway.

She may as well work for her gold jewelry.

"I brought burritos for your lunch, Señorita."

I didn't know what burritos were, but I said, "Thank you. I'll eat after I finish a few more pages."

It took longer than I'd thought to identify an oak wash stand among all the wash stands in the shop, however, and as I was puzzling over which one Luther had indicated in his cashbook, General Pershing came in. He nodded to Yolanda, then he asked, "Has Luther left yet, Cooper?"

I was pleased that he remembered my name. "He left yesterday. He said he'd be back in three or four days."

"Well, possibly nothing will happen before then."

His cautionary tone made my breath catch.

"What might happen?"

He studied me a second before he said, "Huerta's men have crossed into Chihuahua. They chose the wrong side in this revolution, so they have to keep fighting. If they attack Villa, Luther may be caught in the middle of a battle."

He must have seen my concern because he added quickly,

"Don't worry. The federales probably won't reach Aguas de los Caballos before Luther starts back. The infantry on both sides in this conflict are sorry excuses for soldiers, you know, and a battle may be weeks off." He smoothed his brush of a mustache and immediately changed the subject with fake cheerfulness, "The other day, Luther showed me a garnet bracelet. My wife's birthday is coming up, and I might buy it for her."

He spoke too heartily, and my hands shook when I went to the counter and lifted the lid. I didn't ask if his wife genuinely preferred semi-precious stones, and I kept my voice more or less steady while I gave him the bracelet and reached back for the garnet ring. "The stones in this are a good match if your wife might like a ring, too."

He tucked his cap under his arm and weighed the ring and bracelet in his hand a moment before he looked up and smiled. "I'll take them both. Tell Luther I'll bring in the money next week. And I'll wager that one of these days, you'll drive a harder bargain than your grandfather."

He didn't know how dubious that compliment was.

But I merely said, "And you are good at trying to change the subject, General Pershing."

He smiled again. "I really don't see how the federales can reach Villa's headquarters before Luther has returned safely. Both Huerta's and Villa's men would rather loot than fight." He patted my hand. "Keep in mind that the rebels and the whole Mexican army could as easily fade into the hills as mount an attack. There's likely not to be a battle unless they stumble into each other by accident."

He pocketed the ring and bracelet and gave me a hearty wave as he went out.

But he'd been gone no more than a few minutes before I heard a paperboy on the street crying in a mix of English and Spanish, "Una batalla grande! Read all about it. Federal troops y Villa battle near Aguas de los Caballos!"

12

$\mathcal{I}$ GRABBED UP A dollar and ran outside.

"Here!" I called after the boy, who had reached the Bijou sandwich boards and the illustration of Pauline in peril. "I need a paper!"

The little boy wore a man's dress shirt with cut-out sleeves, and his bare feet twinkled under the frayed hem as he turned and loped back to me, the shirt-tail flapping in the wind.

But when I held out the dollar bill, he stiffened. "You have no coins? Un periodico vale two cents, no más. I have no change."

I stood there a moment with the dollar extended toward him. I needed to read about the battle.

The sun poured over us and tanned the little boy's brown arms a few seconds longer before I could get myself to bargain for the first time, but finally I said, "If you let me have this paper now and come back later, I'll get change and pay for five papers."

"Cinco! You want five?"

"I use them for wrapping paper," I alibied.

He narrowed his eyelids at me as if I were deranged, but at last he handed me the newspaper.

"Come back in a hour," I said.

"Sí, Señorita. I will bring the other four papers."

Despite the wind, I stopped on the sidewalk to read the story. The sun baked the top of my head and the gusts threatened to tear the paper out of my hands.

Yolanda stood watching from just inside the door. "What is it, Señorita?"

"General Pershing underestimated the revolutionaries and the army. There was a battle." I went inside and closed out the wind while I scanned down the page. "And it sounds as if the federal men defeated Villa's troops."

She stiffened. "That is not true! Francisco Villa has never been defeated!"

I'd been too impatient, too blunt about her hero, and I offered her the paper. "Well, maybe I read it too fast. You should check out the account yourself."

She merely stared at me for a moment before she tossed her head and turned away. The gold earrings flashed. "General Villa was not defeated! It is a lie if they say there was una derrota."

I realized then that she couldn't read.

I felt a rush of shame.

The day before I'd gloated that even if she blackmailed Luther, she still had to wax furniture. Even that morning I'd resented her gold earrings.

But, of course, the resentment should all have been on her side.

I had all the advantages.

I'd had opportunities she could never dream of. What could a country in the throes of a revolution offer? Luther prided himself on his lineage, and I'd applauded his wealth, but for all I knew Yolanda was a destitute Mexican peasant, lucky to have shoes. She may not even have gone a day to school.

But as much as I wanted to make amends for my earlier harsh judgment, I couldn't think how to read the news aloud without revealing that I knew she was illiterate. If I offered, I'd be pointing out her lack of education. I'd be adding another insult to those I'd already heaped on her in my mind. So I didn't ask if she wanted to hear the story, and we spent the next half hour puttering around the shop without speaking.

Fierce hot blasts howled beyond the window and heated the

room to sweltering, but finally I braved the wind to cross to Miller's
Notions to get change for the paperboy.

When I came back, Yolanda had gone.

I sat down in Luther's favorite chair and re-read the report of the battle near Aguas de los Caballos. But I couldn't get any more from it than the rumors of a defeat for Pancho Villa. Whatever Yolanda wanted to believe, the newspaper reporter had concluded that the federales had won.

When the boy returned for his dime, I hadn't tasted the burritos, and since I couldn't stand the thought of eating in that blast furnace heat, I gave the child my lunch as well as the coin.

"Gracias, Señorita," he said politely, but again he looked at me as if the sun and wind had cooked my brain.

I dawdled in the store until sunset, and when I locked the door, I walked slowly back to the house through the windy dusk. I soon left the streetlights of downtown El Paso behind, but fortunately, many of the mansions on the lane had electric lights glowing from their parlor windows, and I could follow the wooden sidewalk to Luther's driveway.

Naturally no light shone from the windows of my grandparents' house, but as soon as I passed the splashing fountain, I saw the dark figure of Angelica in the black open doorway.

"Yolanda told me there's been a battle," she said in the kind of babyish voice I knew Mary Pickford would have if I ever heard her speak.

I went up the steps with one of the five newspapers under my arm. "The report says that Villa's and the government's men met near Aguas de los Caballos and that the federales defeated Villa's troops."

I held out the paper, but she receded into the even blacker hallway without taking it. "That can't be true," she said. "General Villa's troops have never been defeated. Mr. Harrison says Villa's army is much better equipped than what is left of Huerta's."

I thought, *'He should know.'*

"Mr. Harrison says that *The El Paso Times* always gets things wrong anyway."

I didn't have experience with *The El Paso Times,* so I didn't dispute Luther's assertion as I heard her rustle through the parlor.

I faltered after her to the dining room. Her taffeta wisped and her diamonds glittered as she sank into her chair.

We sat silently through the soup.

But when Yolanda brought in the fish, Angelica said, "Mr. Harrison has always taken care of everything himself."

That had been perfectly obvious from almost the second I arrived.

"His father died, you know, when he was eight."

"I didn't know that."

"At eight years old, he had to support his mother. He's always worked."

I didn't know that either. But it probably explained why he had to control everything.

"He's always said that business should be left to men." Then she surprised me with, "Yet he allowed you to join him at the store." And she astonished me by actually looking at me in the candlelight and waiting for a response.

In my shock that we might actually have a conversation, I took a few seconds to murmur, "I did write and suggest that I could help." When she kept waiting, I added, "And I suppose I don't see anything wrong with women knowing how to run a business."

Her fingers wafted toward the hair ribbon, but her voice lost the little girl quality. "Mr. Harrison would call that a 'Blue Stocking' remark."

I knew 'Blue Stocking' women were suffragettes who drank sherry and smoked cigarettes and argued that females should be able to vote just like men did. Of course Luther would think any competent woman was a 'Blue Stocking.'

And I didn't try to deny that I approved of that kind of female as I said, "I guess I believe girls can learn to do whatever men can do."

"Mr. Harrison would never accept that."

Of course he wouldn't.

"Papa insisted I finish school so I'd be able to support myself even if I never wanted to marry."

After a long pause she said, "I suppose that's the difference in our generations. Every girl in my day knew we had to marry. We understood we had to use our beauty to attract someone who could take care of us."

"Papa believed that women should be able to take care of themselves," I said. "He thought women were just as intelligent as men."

"That may be, but men want beauty when they marry. They don't want intelligence."

"Nonsense." The echo of Luther stopped me cold for a second, and I took a moment to add, "Men want someone to talk to, someone who listens and understands them, just like women do."

"Is that what women want?"

But she immediately dropped the subject by feigning the lisp again and flicking her diamond-encrusted fingers at the *El Paso Times.* "Mr. Harrison would want us to wait for his version of the battle in case one did occur. He should be back in a day or two."

But the next two days went by without a sign of Luther.

Each morning as I unlocked the antique shop, the little boy in the ragged shirt ran up with his stack of morning papers. Each morning, I dutifully paid a dime for five copies.

But for those two days, *The El Paso Times* didn't have any fresh news of General Villa or of General Huerta's federales. There were no additional reports from Chihuahua, and although sometime during the afternoons, I went out and bought a copy of the *Herald* as well, neither daily paper mentioned any Americans near a Chihuahuan battlefield.

They both did report that a General Obregón had marched triumphantly through Mexico City, but since I'd never heard of that general, I didn't know whose side he was on. And was his taking Mexico City good or bad?

The papers also contained the news from France that German General von Kluck had led his army within sight of Paris, and while I read the account, I realized I was having a hard time absorbing the details. The European war raged half a continent and an ocean away, and somehow that conflict had lost its immediacy for me.

I dutifully kept the shop open all day, and occasionally I even sold a piece of furniture for more than Luther had priced in his ledger. As I noted the sale in his cashbook, I put the money in a box that held needles and spools of colored thread. I figured if robbers came in to ransack the safe, they wouldn't bother to search for extra folding money under sewing materials.

But since I was actually just marking time, merely waiting for the reappearance of the wagon, I couldn't revel in being able to take care of the business by myself or in the satisfaction that I, a mere girl, had earned more than Luther would have made on the same sales.

And each dusk, I locked the store and returned through the grit-swirling wind to the dark house that might well have belonged to Sleeping Beauty, festooned with diamonds and lying in a state of suspended animation.

For two nights I didn't sleep well, however.

And on the third morning, I dragged myself out of bed, threw on my clothes, and descended groggily to the dining room where I poked at the tortilla and greasy eggs.

I nonetheless swallowed everything on the plate and finished the dregs of my café con leche before I felt my way through the dark to the entryway and the front door.

The front door consisted of a single ornate panel, carved in a nature pattern of entwined flowers and leaves, and despite its oiled hinges, every morning I had to grapple against the solid weight of the wood.

That morning the mahogany slab seemed heavier than ever, but I finally wrestled it open enough for a shaft of sunshine to fall on the marble entryway.

I gave the handle another hard tug and swung the door wide.

A giant of a man filled the doorway.

13

THE HUGE MAN towered over me. He eclipsed the sun and glared fiercely at me from under a great sombrero that enveloped me in its shadow.

I took a step back.

A black caterpillar eyebrow clung to his forehead, straight across his nose above his black eyes, and a thick black mustache curved over his upper lip and hung in sweeping wings beside his mouth. He wore a filthy once-red kerchief around his neck, and double bandoliers, bristling with ammunition, crossed the expanse of his once-white shirt in a great X. The two holsters riding low on his dirty white cotton trousers held long-barreled pistols with dusty wooden handles. Dust covered the battered cavalry boots that hugged his legs to his knees.

I'd never seen a man so threatening, and I didn't have to speculate this time. I knew for certain I faced a Mexican bandit.

He scowled at me for a long moment, and I expected that any second he'd grab one of the pistols and point it at my head.

I'd hand over the sterling tableware and candlesticks and collect all of Angelica's diamond jewelry without a qualm.

But the bandit didn't move.

Nor did he alter his black scowl or twitch his single black eyebrow, and we stood staring at each other until his lips finally parted under the black mustache and he muttered, "Está la casa de los Harrisons?"

Relieved that he hadn't yet reached for a gun, I stood my ground and forced myself to nod.

"Bueno."

He dug under the knotted scarf into the grubby neck of his filthy, blousy shirt.

I thought for a second he might be merely scratching his chest beneath the soiled cotton, but finally he dragged out a wrinkled envelope and shoved it into my hand.

He continued to scowl at me as he stepped backward off the porch.

He pivoted with military precision and, not giving me another word or a farewell glance, strode away, the spurs on his dusty boots scraping the gravel.

In less than a second, his soiled white shirt and pants, his shoulder cartridge belts, and his dirty sombrero disappeared behind the scratchy green leaves of the cottonwoods. He vanished like smoke.

I took a breath and glanced down at the crumpled envelope.

ANGELICA HARRISON, printed in pencil, slanted across the envelope with unmistakable urgency.

I didn't recognize the handwriting, but somehow I knew the letter came from Luther.

"Yolanda!" I didn't wait to tug the heavy door shut again as I turned and ran through the hall and parlor.

I flung myself headlong through the swinging door into the kitchen.

Light poured in from the high, unshuttered windows, gleamed from the Mexican tile floor, and at a glance, I took in the great wood-burning cook stove, oak icebox, and Yolanda at the sink, scouring an iron skillet.

The back door stood open, and I could see three tiny single-story adobe huts between the house and the stables.

"Yolanda, a letter's come from Señor Harrison! Go tell my grandmother!"

She paled slightly, but she didn't ask anything or object to my
order as she dried her hands against her apron and hurried into the
parlor. The kitchen door swung shut.

Alone in the kitchen, I looked away from the little huts, which I knew were the servants' quarters, inhaled, and tried to control the foreboding that pounded in my chest.

I turned the grimy envelope over in my hands. Angelica's name hadn't been written in Luther's spidery scrawl, but I knew the letter came from him.

There was neither address nor stamp, and I wondered how the Mexican bandit had found the right house.

I stood waiting for what seemed a long time while a bird trilled from somewhere across the yard and the little adobe houses.

Where was Angelica?

Should I rush up to the second floor and find her bedroom?

Should I shout for Yolanda again?

Or should I just rip open the envelope and read the letter myself?

I was still weighing my decision when Angelica appeared—without Yolanda. My grandmother wore the diamond rings on every finger, the diamond studs in her ears, and like a molting stork, she fluttered egret feathers and ecru satin from the elaborate feather boa that cascaded down the front of her peignoir.

The sun reflecting from the Mexican tiles and streaming through the high windows wasn't kind to her thick layer of powder or to her cheeks and lips tinted with rouge, but as I looked at her, I knew she'd once been very beautiful. I also saw why she clung to the diamonds and the shadows, and I knew with absolute certainty why she'd never crossed Texas to see her only son.

"What is it, Cooper?" She cocked her head like a bird.

"It's a letter from Luther." I pressed the envelope into her hand and swallowed the pity that came with the sudden knowledge that she feared exposing her faded beauty to the light, any light. "A Mexican bandit just delivered it."

She didn't take it or ask how I knew the envelope came from Luther as she drew away from the sunlight and me to shrink back into the dining room. I couldn't help observing the fine lines spoking from the corners of her eyes, lacing from her artificially reddened lips. Her feather boa fluttered and settled against the carpet, and for a second the circles of rouge on her cheeks flared fever red. "Why don't you read it to me, Cooper."

I propped the kitchen door ajar with my elbow and undid the scrap of paper. It had been ripped from a child's tablet, scribbled on and then folded into the semblance of an envelope. The inner flap contained the brief note that had no salutation, date, or signature. The words in labored printing sprawled awkwardly across the page.

"Wounded. Will be executed unless ransomed soon. Aguas de los Caballos. 3 right, 12 left, 7 right."

And I suddenly knew that although the note had been addressed to Angelica, Luther had written it to me.

"What does it mean, Cooper?" Angelica's lisp came almost disembodied from the dining room, and I abruptly understood that she reverted to the baby voice when she wanted to avoid hearing or seeing anything unpleasant.

I read the message again in a louder voice.

Despite his predictions about amateurs wandering around in the Mexican desert, Luther himself turned out to be the one kidnapped, the one for whom unreasonable ransoms were evidently being demanded.

"I don't understand."

I read the note for the third time, but my grandmother continued to stare at me in awe.

"I still don't understand," she repeated helplessly.

I looked at her and recited in a single, irate breath, "Luther's been wounded. He must have been caught in that battle between Huerta's men and Villa after all. He says that he'll be executed unless he's ransomed soon."

She didn't move.

"The numbers have to be the combination to the safe."

"A safe?"

I nodded.

"There's no safe in the house."

"It's in the shop behind the counter." I wondered if she'd ever ventured downtown to the shop.

She swayed into a darker corner of the dining room and sank into a chair. Her bejeweled hand lifted, dropped back into her lap. "Mr. Harrison always takes care of everything himself."

"He can't take care of this," I said.

How could she have encased herself in such darkness merely to disguise her aging? How could she pretend helplessness until she became helpless and ignorant? How could she have faked uselessness until she became so utterly useless?

"What is it Mr. Harrison wants, Cooper?"

From the depths of her cave, how could she be expected to understand?

"Luther sent the combination of the safe," I said. "He obviously wants us to take whatever is in the safe to Aguas de los Caballos. Whatever it is may keep him from being shot."

I hadn't meant to blurt out 'may.'

But Angelica didn't seem to notice, "Shouldn't we call General Pershing or General Scott? Isn't keeping people safe on the border part of their job?"

The generals had no clue about the gun-running, and Luther had said that Pershing opposed paying out any ransom for blundering amateurs who might get themselves kidnapped. So I sidestepped with, "I don't think there's time. Luther says he'll be executed 'soon' unless he's ransomed."

"But General Pershing is a good friend to Mr. Harrison. He could send some soldiers into Chihuahua to bring Luther back, couldn't he?"

I stood there, certain he would refuse to risk the lives of American soldiers for a businessman who blatantly ignored his arms embargo. I was equally certain that if we could finally persuade him to go on a rescue mission, it would be too late. So I sidestepped again. "Well, since we don't know when the note was written, I think it would take too long to notify General Pershing and have him order a troop into Mexico." I took a deep breath. "We need to start for Aguas de los Caballos right away."

A shocked silence enveloped the dining room and the kitchen door.

Then Angelica firmed her chin. "We?"

The word hung over us, nearly inaudible, and she gazed at me blankly for a long time before she put on the baby voice again. "You know I couldn't possibly go, Cooper."

I looked at her.

Of course she couldn't go.

"All right," I said. "I can do it."

And as I conceded to do what I'd suspected would happen at the very instant I first read the grubby little letter, I formed a plan for getting the ransom money from Luther's safe—however much it turned out to be—and for conveying it to Aguas de los Caballos.

14

$\mathcal{I}$ COULD ONLY hope I wasn't too late already.

I left Angelica staring after me while I hurried past the dining room table, into the parlor, and through the entryway. I paused at the front door to drag it closed.

My instant strategy included the motion picture people.

Hopefully, they'd been telling me the truth about going to meet Pancho Villa in Chihuahua to make a film. And hopefully, if they actually were from Hollywood, they hadn't yet left the Orndorff Hotel for their journey into Mexico.

If they were still in El Paso and were who they said they were, all I'd have to do was persuade them to let me go with them as far as Aguas de los Caballos.

If they'd merely been making up a good story to fool the locals, I'd have to frame another plan.

I stuffed the scrap of a letter into my skirt pocket as I thudded along the wooden sidewalk and left the dirt street behind me.

The morning desert air hung over the town, still silent and cool, but the mountains rose beyond the outskirts like the smothering rim of a huge dirt bowl.

My side started to ache, but I didn't slow down as I reached the antique store. Nor did I unlock the door. I merely handed a dime to the little boy lounging before the plate glass window. "Leave the newspapers. I'll be back in a minute."

"Sí, Señorita."

I felt him stare after me and shake his head.

My breath came in shorter bursts, and my heart pounded in harder thuds by the time I saw the Orndorff beyond the tree-lined plaza and took one of the diagonal walkways across the square.

In the middle of the plaza, behind a waist-high concrete fence, an attendant tossed something from a bucket to three alligators.

So Eduardo Jimenez hadn't been lying about seeing alligators in the plaza.

If only he'd also been telling the truth about himself.

The uniformed attendant didn't glance in my direction as I ran past. He kept a wary eye on the six-foot-long alligators while he stayed close to the fence and threw what looked like haunches of beef toward the three pairs of jaws.

I barely paused at the edge of the plaza to let a Packard drive by before I dashed across the street and into the hotel.

A lone night clerk stood behind the desk, watching me as I clicked over the black and white tiles toward him.

"Are Eduardo Jimenez and Matt Gordon still registered in the hotel?"

The clerk, a pimpled boy maybe my age, stared at me haughtily. "Only visitors on a authorized list is allowed to see our guests," he said grandly. "I ain't authorized to give out that information."

I stopped directly in front of him and let my breath catch up with me.

I couldn't afford the delay of a hassle any more than I could afford to watch the alligators, but since I needed to know immediately if Eduardo Jimenez had left the hotel or not, I summoned a cold grandeur that topped the pimpled boy's. "If you don't tell me in the next ten seconds whether Eduardo Jimenez is still registered and is still in the hotel, I'll raise a ruckus you won't believe."

He hadn't practiced haughtiness enough to maintain it under that kind of threat, and his cool expression shriveled.

"The day manager ain't come in yet. You want to see him, you go wait over there. He's the one to say who's still registered and who's still in the hotel."

"In ten seconds I'm going to start shouting and banging on doors. It's six o'clock in the morning, and I don't think your hotel guests will appreciate the hollering and yelling they're going to wake up to. One thousand one, one thousand two—"

"Mr. Jimenez and Mr. Gordon is still in the hotel. Top floor suite," he said in a rush of panic. He grabbed up the telephone. "Room 406. I'll ring."

It occurred to me that he might be calling the house detective to have me thrown out, but I didn't peg him for that brand of quick thinking, so I let him ring, and when he asked, "What's your name?" I told him.

He repeated my name into the phone, listened, then nodded to me. "Go on up."

An elevator attached to thick wires and pulleys sat waiting behind a scrolled iron gate, but I'd always felt a little claustrophobic in elevators, so I veered toward the broad marble staircase at the end of the lobby. And just in case the clerk came to his senses and did call the house detective, I took the stairs two at a time.

I reached the door to Suite 406 just as it swung open.

Eduardo Jimenez walked into the hall, not in a costume this time but in an ordinary pair of trousers, suspenders, and a striped red and white shirt with a celluloid collar. "I thought I r-recognized your name."

He backed up for me to follow him into the suite.

The older man came from one of the bedrooms, attaching a celluloid collar to his shirt and scowling.

I suspected that if handsome Eduardo Jimenez really were an actor, Matt Gordon had to chase girls away from him all the time, but this morning, the cameraman's disapproval wasn't about to deter me, and I said at once, "I hope you were telling me the truth about being from Hollywood and about going into Mexico to make a film of General Villa." I didn't give either of them a chance to answer. "When are you leaving?"

Eduardo flashed his dimples. "We're leaving as s-soon as we can get a railway ticket to Chihuahua City."

"The trains on the Mexico Central ain't exactly regular right now," Matt Gordon said.

"You have to expect some d-disruption in the middle of a revolution, Matt," Eduardo said with disarming sweetness.

I hadn't thought ahead enough to decide what I'd do if I found them. I'd only hoped they turned out to be who they said they were and that I could find them. But in that instant I concocted another full-blown plan. "I have a car."

They both gave me a puzzled stare, the kind Angelica had given me, and I added quickly, "It's my grandfather's Ford. There's plenty of room for your camera equipment. We can drive it into Mexico together, and then—"

"Drive into Mexico together!" Matt Gordon's fingers fell away from the collar fasteners.

I pulled the scribbled note from my pocket. "My grandfather's been kidnapped. I don't know whether bandits or federales captured him, but I have to deliver ransom to whoever's holding him as soon as possible. Otherwise, they're going to shoot him."

"How old are you? Fourteen?" Matt Gordon sputtered. "Taking a fourteen-year-old girl into Mexico would be—"

"I'm fifteen."

"—would be the stupidest move anybody in his right mind—"

"I can drive, but I figured that if we all went together, you wouldn't have to wait for the train, and I could—"

"No!"

"My grandfather will be shot by his kidnappers unless I reach him in time. I have to go whether you come with me or not."

Eduardo Jimenez gazed at me with sympathy. His dark brown

eyes held a velvety kindness, and I also suspected he gazed sympathetically at most people. "Matt—" he began.

"No! I promised your mother I'd watch out for you, and this is one sure way to get us both killed or jailed."

"General Pershing is a friend of my grandfather's, and he says—"

"You're a fifteen-year-old girl!"

"General Pershing says the government troops have to keep fighting. They have to keep attacking Villa's army. This could be the perfect time to film a battle. In daylight like Pancho Villa promised."

As I blurted out all of that, I told myself I hadn't actually lied by saying there would be a battle.

But before Matt Gordon could object again, Eduardo said, "We wouldn't have to wait here until doomsday, Matt. Especially if there's going to be a b-battle. We could meet General Villa and get this over with. We could be home in time for Mother's birthday."

"I ain't about to risk your life and mine in some harebrained—"

"It won't take more than a day to get to Aguas de los Caballos if we take the Ford," I said.

Luther had calculated he could leave El Paso in the morning and reach the town by nightfall, and he'd been driving a heavy wagon, so surely we could do it in a day driving a truck.

"Having our own transportation might even be safer than taking the train into Chihuahua," I added quickly, telling myself I hadn't actually said it would be safer.

"I'll wire Ben," Eduardo seconded at once. "You know how happy he'll be to know we're going into Mexico at last and getting some battle film to send him. And I can wire Mother we're meeting General Villa and that we'll be back in time for her party."

I could see he had Matt Gordon's attention.

"If we leave here by noon, we'll reach Aguas de los Caballos by tomorrow morning," I said with great conviction, hoping it was true, while I started toward the door. "I'll be at the antique store. The truck is parked there, and we can get started right away. Come as soon as you're ready."

I hurried into the hall before Matt Gordon could raise further objections that would force me to side-step some more or make me tell a downright lie.

I clattered down the marble stairs.

By that time, a few other guests milled around the lobby, but I didn't glance at them—or at the boy desk clerk—as I raced outside and crossed the plaza.

The attendant still stood inside the fence at the alligator pool tossing the chunks of bloody meat to the alligators, and it was as if I hadn't been gone long at all.

It had seemed an eternity.

And I realized that it also seemed as if I'd been in El Paso for years.

When I reached the antique shop, I scooped up the five papers, then unlocked and relocked the door. I didn't turn on the lights or flip the CLOSED placard as I ran to the telephone, dialed, and asked for number 417.

I estimated that seven or eight days should give me time to locate Luther, no matter who held him, and drive back to El Paso, so when Yolanda answered the phone, I said, "I need you to pack enough food for a week."

"Señorita?"

"Enough food to last a week. I don't care what it is."

I omitted mention of the two Hollywood people since I didn't have time to explain, and I tried to remember what else Luther had told her to pack. "And water. I'll need plenty of water. Fruit and boiled eggs, and some matches and candles. Bring everything to the store."

I heard myself giving orders—just like Luther.

"Tell my grandmother I'm going to Aguas de los Caballos with the ransom right away. I'm taking the Tin Lizzie, and I have to start as soon as possible, so hurry!"

I hung up before she could ask any questions.

Then I took out Luther's note again and knelt before the safe.

Luther, as the keeper of secrets, hadn't wanted me even to glimpse what he'd locked in his steel vault. And I'd have stayed ignorant if kidnappers hadn't forced his hand.

Only when his life depended on it, did he concede to share the combination.

If that's what the cryptic numbers in the note stood for, of course.

I held my breath and twisted the knob.

The incised numbers clicked into place with ease, and when I gave the dial a last turn to the right and stopped at seven, the heavy door swung open.

15

I PUSHED THE METAL door all the way back and peered inside the safe.

The lower shelf held two bulging suede sacks, but only a crude wooden cheese box sat on the top shelf.

So Luther's most secret loot consisted of two sacks and a cheap wooden box.

I lifted out one bag, got up, and clunked it onto the counter. I remembered the sacks of corn while I reached down for the other bag and hefted it to the counter top as well.

Then I untied the leather thong that knotted the first sack and tipped it on its side.

Gold disks spilled across the glass.

Coins spun from the mouth of the bag, some as tiny as my pinkie nail, some the size of coat buttons, some a good two inches across—all of them featuring the embossed profiles of monarchs with crowns and scepters or beautiful bas-relief birds and animals. A flat gold rectangle the size of my palm tumbled out, and I recognized it as one the famous pirate 'pieces of eight' from a picture I'd seen in an encyclopedia.

Luther had amassed a fortune in antique coins.

But now we—both Luther and I—had a problem.

How much would such an accumulation of ancient gold bring on the market?

Luther had deliberately kept me in the dark, and now I couldn't even guess what the tidy mountain of gold would be worth.

I took a shaky breath and shoved that pile aside.

I undid the second sack and poured it out on the countertop.

This suede bag held only Theodore Roosevelt Indian-head gold pieces, burnished, sparkling, and in mint condition—just like the one Rosalie Boudreaux had tucked into Mama's beaded purse the morning I left New Orleans.

Rosalie's gift had been beautiful and thoughtful, and I'd thought at the time that I wouldn't spend it. I'd debated framing it in a little shadow box, despite the fact that I could have bought a new dress and a matching pair of shoes with it. I'd traced my fingertips over the imperial Indian chieftain on one side and the fierce eagle on the reverse while I remembered the good things about Rosalie and New Orleans.

And now, as I stared down at the coins from Luther's sack, each a replica of mine, I knew that each had a value of five dollars.

Well, at least I could tabulate how much this pile of gold amounted to.

I deftly separated the coins into columns of ten and ended up with exactly twenty glittering stacks. Luther had bagged a thousand dollars of new coins, enough to pay for a couple of new automobiles.

I stood there looking at the tumble of foreign antique coins and the golden columns of recently minted money. He'd had to relinquish the combination of the safe, but which coins had he intended for me to take into Mexico?

How much money would keep him from being executed? What unreasonable, exorbitant fee—which Jack Pershing would never approve—would ransom him?

I had no clue about what he'd been trying to tell me between the penciled lines that weren't in his handwriting.

I inhaled another breath.

Well, if he had to use this hidden stash to free himself from his captors, so be it.

I'd take it all.

But that brought up another problem.

How could I be certain of reaching Aguas de los Caballos with any of it?

If government troops occupied Aguas de los Caballos and held Luther captive, I might run into General Villa's men before I reached the village. I'd been amply warned that Pancho Villa wouldn't hesitate to steal from anyone. So how could I ransom Luther from the federales if Villa found the money first?

But if General Villa's soldiers controlled the town and Luther, what would prevent government soldiers from stopping the pie wagon and seizing the gold before the Hollywood people and I even got close to Aguas de los Caballos?

My next breath stopped before it got to my lungs and my heart accelerated while I improvised another instant plan. At least I could give myself two chances.

I scooped all the foreign coins back into their bag and retied the thong.

Then I hurried into the storeroom and grabbed a red and blue blanket off the shelf.

As I came back, I unfolded the scratchy wool and spread it out on the counter beside the stacks of Roosevelt coins. I got down the box of sewing things under which I'd been hiding store sales, and threaded a needle.

I laid a five-dollar gold piece on the blanket edge and sewed a cross over it, side to side, top to bottom.

Mama had always poked fun at me whenever I'd tried to sew, and now I saw that my stitches, as usual, were coming out uneven and awkward.

But since I didn't aim for neatness, I worked as fast as possible, spacing the gold discs and pulling the thread taut so the coins wouldn't budge.

I stitched, tied off each cross as I finished it, and when I had an entire edge lined with gold pieces, I folded the glistening border over and hemmed the red and blue plaid wool in place.

It would be the clumsiest, thousand-dollar blanket in the world, but no clink would betray the gold.

I kept sewing, constantly rethreading the needle and depleting the columns of five-dollar coins while I secured them along each edge of the blanket.

At last, as I was hemming the final gold piece into the final side, Yolanda appeared in the front window with a market basket and a ten-quart metal can.

She wore the gold earrings and her straw sombrero.

Didn't she realize we didn't have any time to waste? Had she given any thought to Luther when she paused to put on her earrings?

She was as bad as Angelica with her diamonds.

But at any rate, she'd come to the shop in time.

I tried to control my irritation while I knotted and cut the thread, and ran to unlock the door.

I grabbed the hamper and carried it to the counter. "Close the door," I said over my shoulder as I took up the lumpy sack of antique coins and shoved the suede bag down the wicker side of the basket.

Then I folded the plaid blanket, which was even heavier than I'd anticipated, while I tried to be offhanded and casual.

Yolanda lugged the heavy can to the counter while I bent to lock the safe again.

I'd nearly forgotten the stupid cheese box still on the top shelf, but now I took it out and pushed the thin slat lid along its dovetail grooves.

The rough-hewn interior of the box had been crammed with crystalline stones, some cut with round, multi-faceted bases that tapered to flawless points, some cut into facets of rectangles or squares. They all shone with hypnotic brilliance.

Yolanda peered over the counter into the box. "Oh, Señorita, aren't they beautiful!"

Of course they weren't crystals, they were diamonds.

And of course, they, not the gold, were Luther's real passion, his real treasure.

With which he'd created one more problem for me.

Did he want me to carry any of them into Mexico for his ransom?

"Oh, all right," I said aloud as I made another lightning choice.

"Señorita?"

"I'll take some."

"Señorita?"

She stared at me as I scooped out half a dozen loose stones, not choosing sizes or shapes, just grabbing the first six my hand touched. I held them in my fist while I slid the cover shut again and shoved the box back in the safe. With my free hand, I slammed the safe door and whirled the dial.

Then I twisted the lid off the water can and, without looking at the diamonds again, I dropped them in the water.

I recapped the can just as Eduardo Jimenez and Matt Gordon staggered through the door with satchels, suitcases, and an elaborate contraption on a tripod that I recognized as a movie camera.

As they burst inside with the wind, Yolanda gasped.

"They're all right," I said. "They're going with me to find Luther."

"Where's the car?" Matt Gordon panted.

"Around back."

I grabbed up the key to the front door and handed it to Yolanda. "Bring the water can," I said.

Then I lifted the basket and weighty blanket to lead the way through the storeroom.

After I unlocked that door, and Matt Gordon and Eduardo filed into the sunlight with their equipment, I gave Yolanda the storeroom key and took the water can from her. "Get me two more blankets and that dipper." I pointed my chin toward the shelves

While she did as I asked, I realized I hadn't been adding 'please,' and I felt my face grow hot. Even if it felt like I'd lived on the border for years, I hadn't been in El Paso more than a few days. But already I mimicked my grandparents' rudeness.

"Be sure to lock the door after us when we leave."

"Sí, Señorita."

I'd done it again.

To lessen my flush I wished I could have added that we'd bring Luther back. But I knew how false that assurance would echo if it fell out of my mouth, so I didn't say it, and I waited a lame pause before I said, "I forgot to ask you to bring me a hat. Could you let me borrow yours?"

She started. "Oh, no!"

I opened my mouth for a 'please,' but she said, "Neither the Señora nor Señor Harrison would approve of you wearing the hat of a campesino, Señorita."

Of course she was right. My grandparents did fancy themselves aristocrats.

But I couldn't afford to have her insist on both of us going along with their tiresome snobbery, so I added quickly, "Why don't you wear the hat that's on the dresser in my room until I get back."

She gazed at me a second.

"It belonged to my mother."

For the first time, she gave me a small smile. "If that is what you wish, Señorita Cooper."

She untied the straw hat, took it off, and tucked it under my arm.

When I murmured, "Gracias," she nodded. Then she said, "Señora Harrison wishes you good luck."

I felt a sudden tightening of my throat as if someone had pulled a string hard around my neck.

We were all going to need all the luck we could get.

16

*M*ATT GORDON AND Eduardo Jimenez stood staring at the ungainly vehicle with HARRISON AND ROBARTS ANTIQUES on the side of the awkward wooden enclosure.

"I forgot to ask if you could drive," I said as Yolanda and I went outside. "But if you both know how, we can take turns at the wheel."

Matt Gordon jerked his thumb toward Eduardo. "His mother's got a chauffeur," he said. "So he ain't drove all that much."

Eduardo blushed.

"Well, that probably doesn't matter," I said. The driving I'd done in Papa's Model T hadn't been all that complicated, and I added to ease Eduardo's embarrassment, "A Ford isn't hard to maneuver."

I put the water can and basket down beside the pile of equipment next to the car before I took the plaid blankets from Yolanda and laid them with mine in the back seat. Then I unlatched the double doors. "We can put all this stuff in the back. We don't want to worry about it while we drive across the desert."

I half expected Matt Gordon to balk at taking orders from a fifteen-year-old girl, but he didn't, and both he and Eduardo seemed to accept that I knew where we were going and what we were going to do when we got there.

And neither of them objected to packing equipment on the tonneau floor mat of the truck.

Yolanda watched us a moment before she said softly, "Vaya con Dios, Señorita."

When she went back inside, I heard the key to the storeroom click with finality.

I took a deep breath, pulled her crumpled straw sombrero over my curls, and tied the ribbon under my chin. Her peasant hat fit me perfectly.

Matt Gordon and Eduardo shuttled back and forth, and since I'd always been good at judging spaces, I shoved things around, wedging smaller boxes between larger pieces of luggage and making room for the basket, suitcases, camera, and film. I kept the water can close to the doors.

The packing was hot and sweaty work, and it took longer than it should have, but finally everything was stowed, and we each gulped down half a dipper of water.

I listened for the tick of diamonds rolling around the can, but I couldn't hear anything over the rattle of the dipper. And I could tell that diamonds didn't taste.

"Who wants to drive first?" I latched the back doors. "Do we know which road to take?"

Eduardo nodded. "I looked at the map Villa sent the studio. We can follow the road along the railroad track. Straight into Aguas de los Caballos."

The knotted string around my neck tightened.

Who would control Aguas de los Caballos when we got there?

"I'll drive first," Matt Gordon volunteered before he turned to Eduardo. "You handle the starter lever while I crank. As soon as the motor catches, I'll take over."

"All right then. Let's go." As I climbed onto the running board, I hoped I still sounded confident.

But before I could analyze the echo of my words, Eduardo

appeared beside me and gave me a gentlemanly hand to aid my balance.

A spark of impatience replaced the tremor in my chest, and I was tempted to knock his hand away.

Surely he wasn't going to display that kind of stupid courtesy while we drove across northern Mexico. I wasn't lame or old, and I certainly didn't need anyone's assistance to get into a car.

But at the moment it was both easier and faster to let him help than to argue, so I grabbed his hand and clambered into the back seat.

I let his fingers go, sat down, and tucked my skirt around the tops of my boots. Only then did I notice I'd matched a pair of blue stockings to my blue sash that morning.

I watched Eduardo slide behind the steering wheel and try to rub his fingers without my noticing, and I realized my irritation had made my grip pretty fierce.

Well, maybe that would stop his ridiculous chivalry.

Matt Gordon hunkered down before the hood of the pie wagon to work the crank. The gray fedora bobbed up and down as he turned the handle.

"I remember how to get to the bridge that crosses the Rio Grande." I raised my voice over the whine of the crank. "I can get us into Mexico."

"F-fine." Eduardo kept his gaze glued to the pedals and the choke.

Matt Gordon cranked until at last the motor sputtered to a start and rumbled with a vibrating hum. Eduardo eased quickly across to the passenger side, and I caught a glimpse of a holster and the silver-handled pistol he wore under the driving duster.

As if that would be of any use to us.

Matt Gordon came around the hood and jumped behind the steering wheel. He released the brake, and we started to roll.

I shouted to his celluloid collar that rose above his tan duster, "Go through the alley and turn left on the first street."

We picked up speed and emerged from the alley onto the paved street without slowing down. Matt Gordon honked furiously. A horse pulling a buggy shied out of our way, and the driver in a checkered suit and derby yelled at us.

It was just as well we couldn't hear him over the motor, and I thought that even Eduardo with his inexperience could probably have driven as well as Matt Gordon.

"Turn right," I shouted.

In no time we lunged over the trolley tracks and then past the red brick station and beside the barbed wire fence glittering along the banks of the river.

Half a dozen soldiers in American uniforms lounged beside the length of fence, and I thought it might be comforting to have a corporal or two traveling with us.

It was dumb to wish for that, however, and I consciously looked away from the soldiers.

In a few seconds, we wobbled onto the ramp of the Stanton Street Bridge that spanned the river, and as the wheels thudded against the uneven planks we were thrown around the truck. Eduardo and I grabbed the metal sides of the Tin Lizzie to keep from being pitched out, and Matt clutched the steering wheel while he stared through the windshield and accelerated.

Pedestrians, strolling over the wooden bridge toward Juarez in a holiday spirit even though it was a weekday, jumped out of our way, and a few of them shouted after us. The driver of an open-air excursion car, carrying sightseers across the river, swerved his donkeys to keep the pie wagon from smashing into them.

That driver yelled at us, too, as we jolted around the excursion car with its sign on the side, VISIT OLD MEXICO, and whizzed past.

Matt Gordon hurtled us toward the glassed-in kiosk on the Mexico side of the bridge manned by two uniformed attendants. He made no effort to slow the Tin Lizzie, and I thought the men in uniform might not only shout at us but start shooting as we sped by.

Neither Mexican border guard gave us more than a perfunctory glance, however, as we reached the kiosk, passed the glass booth, and lurched off the bridge into Mexico.

The dirt street, with a sign on the corner that read Calle Comercio, was jammed with pedestrians and wagons, and it became immediately obvious that if Matt Gordon didn't want to smash into the crowd and get us thrown in jail for manslaughter, he had to slow down.

Fortunately, that thought must have occurred to him as well, and at last he jerked on the hand brake. Eduardo braced himself as he lunged against the dashboard, and I slammed hard into the back of the driver's seat.

But at least I could stop holding my breath.

The motor nearly stalled, and Matt Gordon stomped on pedals and manipulated levers to keep the engine from choking off as the pie wagon shuddered to a crawl. The crowd surged in on it from all sides, but everyone ignored us as if we'd merely parked in the middle of the street.

Indian-stoic women in dusty black dresses and bare feet wove around us while they balanced panniers of tortillas on their rolled braids. Butchers in leather aprons carried dripping slabs of meat over their shoulders, and mustached farmers ignored us as they plowed their way through the peasants with great trays of tomatoes and purple onions.

Only the tattered children who held up begging palms at the sides of the Tin Lizzie acknowledged us.

Eduardo glanced back at me with an apologetic expression as he began to distribute pennies and nickels into the filthy little hands.

I knew as well as he did that visitors to foreign countries weren't supposed to encourage beggars, but since I'd probably have done the same thing if I'd had the presence of mind to bring any change, I didn't try to reprimand him.

Matt Gordon crept along so slowly now that the children ran along beside us, stretching their arms toward us until Eduardo at last ran out of coins.

Then the tiny beggars finally dropped behind to find new marks as we inched past dirty stucco storefronts that advertised tequila. Well-dressed men in fedoras and suits edged around the peasant women and pan-handlers to dodge in and out of the cantinas, and elaborately costumed men on horseback rode with impassive faces down the center of the dirt street. Other automobiles criss-crossed before our front bumper, the drivers honking and gesturing and forcing us to pause before stalls long enough for the proprietors to run out and offer us concho belts and silver bracelets.

I kept shaking my head and repeating, "No gracias, amigo" into the hot, dry air that was thick with the odor of chiles.

We passed a block of buildings whose adobe showed hundreds of gouges, and Eduardo turned around and pointed to the bullet-splattered walls. He shouted, "These were damaged when General Villa's men captured Juarez."

I nodded.

Hopefully General Villa's men had also captured Aguas de los Caballos. With perhaps less damage.

Matt Gordon drove slowly along until at last the shops and cafés thinned out, the crowd dwindled, and we reached a rococo mission church surrounded by dying cottonwoods. Only a few old women in black shawls loitered on the church steps, and when we passed the railway station a few blocks beyond the elaborate church façade, no one seemed to be tending the ticket booth or supervising the flatcars and engines waiting on the sidings.

I hoped Eduardo and Matt Gordon appreciated the fact that no trains were running.

But just then Eduardo pointed toward a road that ran beside
the tracks, and Matt Gordon turned onto it.

He picked up speed again, and a great column of powdered dirt formed, thickened behind us as we left the town and followed the road into the dry mesquite.

The road of course was no more than parallel ruts, spaced for wagon wheels rather than for cars, and the high yellow grass that grew between the baked stripes of earth whipped the underside of the Ford. The curve of the beaten tracks followed the rails toward the arid brown peaks at the horizon, and telegraph poles rose at regular intervals between the railroad and the path.

Sagebrush and brown paltry-leaved bushes dotted the landscape and a few sprigs of yellow grass that looked like broom-straw sprouted from the outcroppings of stone. Transparent ribbons of heat wavered up from the parched ground and made the row of telegraph poles dance.

We were off.

And even if I was only fifteen, Matt Gordon and Eduardo Jimenez trusted that I could guide them to Pancho Villa's headquarters and get us back to El Paso again.

The thud in my skull accelerated with the speed of the truck. Panic surged over me, and my tongue dried to powdered brick.

I didn't know a thing about the semi-desert land we'd entered except that it got cold at night. I wouldn't recognize a rattlesnake if we ran over one.

And I couldn't even guess about what might come next.

17

THE PIE WAGON whirled along the dirt road, and dust exploded behind it.

Of course all the grit didn't stay behind the truck, and when I wiped my shaking hand across my forehead, I might as well have been dragging sandpaper over my skin.

I tried to steady my fingers as I adjusted the ribbon on Yolanda's sombrero and tapped Matt Gordon on the shoulder. "Want me to spell you?"

"I'm okay." He raised his voice, but he kept his eyes on the parallel tracks and the center of grass as if he would take a wrong turn unless he watched them closely.

Eduardo glanced at me and grinned while he took a white handkerchief from his pocket and mopped his face.

Despite his misplaced chivalry that would make me squirrelly if I had to be around him much, he was handsome, and during the next few minutes that I sat observing his good-looking profile I felt less apprehensive.

I took a breath and told myself we might have a chance to rescue Luther.

And after we got back to El Paso, I'd inform Luther that I didn't see anything wrong with movies. I'd tell him that I intended to go to the pictures whenever I felt like it. Eduardo had modestly averred that *The Life of Pancho Villa* would be good even if he starred in it, and I certainly would buy a ticket to it when it came to the Bijou.

I also decided on the spot that I'd buy Yolanda a ticket, too.

I leaned against the seat, watched Eduardo return the handkerchief to the pocket of his duster, and realized that I no longer had to blame—or justify—Yolanda for blackmailing Luther.

In fact, when I opened his safe and found that hoard of gold and gems, I concluded—without actually reasoning it out—that she more than deserved whatever she got from him. And since he behaved so shabbily to his servants and his horses—and Angelica—Yolanda might at least get something extra for being treated as an inferior.

Just then, Matt Gordon pointed to a shape wavering through the heat oscillations. "What's that?"

I could tell what it was at once.

A man hung from the crosstree of a telegraph pole.

As we sped by the body, I saw that the man's wrists had been tied behind him, and that his dead weight dragged cement-heavy from the rope around his neck. He wore only tattered cotton trousers, and his bare chest and bare feet had dried to cracked leather in the sun. I couldn't tell through the dust, but I thought his eyeballs had been plucked out.

I exhaled and gripped the metal edge of the truck.

Eduardo shook his head in sympathy as he turned away.

Neither of us looked back.

The dust whirled and the transparent ribbons of heat wavered mirages ahead.

We thudded over the bumpy path in silence until finally the sun began to drop lower in the white sky.

In a little while I detected pink streaks in the clouds, the sun turned blood orange, and at last the great red disk reached the jagged peaks on the horizon. As it disappeared behind the mountains, Matt Gordon swerved aside from the railroad tracks and stopped.

He pulled hard on the brake, and the pie wagon sat vibrating with inertia for a few seconds. Then Eduardo jumped to the ground to help me unwind from the back seat.

My impatience flared again.

I wanted to snarl at him that he wasted our time with those silly trappings of gentility. I was certainly no swooning damsel and I could have helped him down as easily as he could help me.

But then I reminded myself he wasn't Luther. He was a boy who bought birthday presents for his mother. And maybe his mother insisted that he hand girls down from automobiles.

I controlled my impulse to snap at him, and I let him take my hand while I tried not to crunch his fingers this time.

When he went with me to help unlatch the back doors of the truck, I again managed to stay calm. I took a breath and let him lift out the heavy water can.

As I'd expected, he twisted off the lid and gallantly offered me the dipper.

My throat had baked dry, and the first mouthful of water felt like a steel cube forcing its way through my esophagus.

"You okay?"

I grimaced, but finally swallowed and handed him the dipper. "I'm okay."

While he and Matt Gordon took their sips of water, I dragged out the basket, set it on the pebbles of washed-away topsoil, and rummaged for the box of matches. I went to the front of the truck and lit one of the kerosene lanterns before Eduardo could run up to help. As I trimmed the wick and the yellow light glowed on the desert floor, I experienced another surge of optimism.

I felt sure for a second that we would find Luther.

But after I passed around the packet of burritos and Matt Gordon settled himself on a large rock to ask, "How much farther to Aguas de los Caballos?" I was jolted again with the fact that I had no idea.

My contentment evaporated. I nonetheless sat down on the running board beside Eduardo and said stoutly, "We should be there by noon."

I didn't want either of them to pursue that, however, so I foraged quickly for another topic and said to Eduardo, "I've been wondering. Won't it be hard to play a real person? With an actual person like Pancho Villa, don't you have to know him?"

He gave me that kind, dimpled smile. "What you have to do is identify what makes him vulnerable."

When I nodded, he added, "It also helps if you can admire a personality trait in him that you'd like to have yourself."

"And you found something in Villa to admire?"

"I've read everything I could find about him and the Revolution. He actually seems a rather good sort."

That sounded like something Papa would say.

I couldn't accuse Eduardo of being as innocent as my clergyman father, however, and I let the conversation lapse while we finished the burritos.

Then I got out a wire container of boiled eggs and a mesh bag of figs, and Eduardo said, "Have you read *Tarzan of the Apes?* Our picnic here in the open could almost be one of those elegant dinners in the jungle."

That seemed a safe enough topic, and I said, "I'm halfway through, so don't tell me the ending."

He laughed. "When I grow enough hair on my chest to play the part of Tarzan, I'm going to p-persuade Mars Studio to film the story."

What other boy would admit so casually he didn't have hair on his chest?

I peered at him in the kerosene light. "How old are you?"

"I'll be sixteen in November."

No wonder he seemed naive. No wonder he kept trying to act grown-up and urbane. I'd probably been right about the fact that he didn't shave yet either.

"When I convince the studio to make the picture, why don't you come to Hollywood and audition for J-Jane?"

He was obviously flirting with me. But he did it so awkwardly that I snorted.

And then I added something I didn't know I was going to add, something I didn't even know I'd concluded. "I'm going to be an antique dealer, not an actress. I'd much rather sit in a theatre and be entertained than see myself on screen."

For a second he gazed at me with undisguised admiration. "Few people can articulate so positively what they want to be."

I dismissed that, too. "I suppose you're right."

But he was right.

I did know what I wanted to be. While I followed Luther around that first morning in the shop I discovered that I loved antiques. And after a couple of days, I knew it wouldn't be hard to make a fortune from them. I wouldn't be like Luther, however, and lose my son because I was a crook. I'd make my profits decently, honestly. I'd identify not just what made people vulnerable, but what they yearned for, and I'd persuade them to buy oak chairs that matched their oak tables. I'd supply the elegance they desired.

I didn't need to say that aloud in the Mexican desert, however, and I asked instead, " How about you? Did you always want to be a movie star?"

"Oh, yes. My mother's an actress. I've been doing scenes with her from the time I was two."

And trying to act like an adult from the time you were eight.

"She's more talented than M-Mary Pickford."

Matt Gordon wiped his fingers on a tuft of grass and extracted a cigarette from a gold case. He took up the box of matches, lit the cigarette, and exhaled a perfect circle of smoke. "His mother's the most beautiful actress in Hollywood."

His hyperbole betrayed him. Was he in love with Eduardo's mother?

I didn't know how Eduardo might feel about that, or if he even wanted to acknowledge it, and since I was becoming really good at pretending not to notice things, I included Matt Gordon as I asked, "Have you seen Mary Pickford in person?"

"Oh, s-sure."

"Her studio is just down the street," Matt Gordon seconded. But his voice was too casual, and I could tell he knew he'd given himself away. He was in love with Eduardo's mother.

"Mary Pickford is really tiny, but they also b-build the sets for her larger than life so she'll look even smaller."

"They do?"

"It's all illusion, you know."

In the silence, Matt Gordon blew another perfect, but too casual, circle of smoke and said, "How about we get some rest? Ain't we starting as soon as it's light?"

"Of c-course."

I stood up. "It'll cool down tonight. So I brought blankets."

I reached in the back seat for the two extras, handed them to Eduardo, and climbed into the truck before he could push around me to do the polite gesture.

I unfolded my ungainly blanket, and as I draped the gold-laden hem around my shoulders, Eduardo puffed out the car lantern.

He and Matt Gordon immediately became indistinct wraiths in the dark.

"G-good-night."

I couldn't see much from beneath the truck roof, but the stars low on the horizon seemed huge and clear and close enough to gather in my fist. I curled up on the back seat under the awkward blanket and studied the strange midnight blue-green of the sky.

Eduardo Jimenez and Matt Gordon, who loved Eduardo's mother, were depending on me.

I lay looking at the glittering clusters of stars and told myself to make a plan.

But how could I plan when I didn't know where Aguas de los Caballos actually was or what might be there if we located it? And how could I plan for a quick return trip to El Paso even if I did find Luther right away?

I'd essentially promised Matt Gordon a battle he could photograph in daylight, but since of course I had no control over Pancho Villa's skirmishes, we might have to stay in Mexico a long time before the government forces attacked Villa or he attacked them.

I closed my eyes for a second.

Then something bumped hard against the side of the Tin Lizzie, and my eyes jerked open again.

The stars had vanished. A gray dome curved over the mountains at the horizon.

And a dozen mustached faces, sheltered by dark hat brims, stared down at me.

18

I SAT UP SLOWLY, trying to get my bearings in the dawn light.

A ring of solemn men surrounded the pie wagon. Beyond them, a circle of horses impatiently stamped their hooves and exhaled steam.

All the men cradled rifles and glittered with bandoliers strapped in great Xs across their chests, but their clothes ranged from mismatched suits and filthy white cottons to filthier serapes, worn with such a motley assortment of fedoras and sombreros that I concluded in an instant that they weren't government troops.

We'd been overtaken by bandits.

But were they Pancho Villa's bandits?

I glanced toward Matt Gordon and Eduardo. They sat on the ground beside the pie wagon, half tangled in the plaid blankets, looking as startled and groggy as I felt.

The bandits stared at us in silence for a long time.

Finally one of them, a short man with gray mustache drooping over his upper lip and a scarlet muffler wrapped around his neck, broke the silence and jabbed his rifle butt into the basket beside the truck fender. "Que tienes, hombres?"

He kicked the basket over.

Yolanda's carefully tied bundles spilled from the wicker mouth, and the eggs scattered, cracking on washed-up stones. A net bag of limes and the mesh sacks of oranges and figs rolled out along with the matches and half a dozen candles bound with string. At last the heavy sack of gold tumbled from the hamper.

"Que tienes?" the gray-haired bandit repeated as he stirred everything around with the toe of his boot. He peered down and separated the cloth bundles and the fruit from the lumpy suede bag.

I watched him nudge the sack of gold with his foot, and even though I was pretty sure most females in Mexico kept silent in the company of men, I blurted, "We're trying to find General Villa's headquarters. Is Aguas de los Caballos very far away?"

Just as I'd thought, the man eyed me with astonishment, as if the last thing he expected was for a girl to speak. His mouth gaped under the gray mustache.

Eduardo took a breath and glanced at me with his apologetic expression before he repeated my question in Spanish.

I was slightly gratified that no one answered him either.

In the silence the horses puffed and jingled reins and bits. Then the short, gray-haired man gestured to a wispy-looking man in a striped blue suit.

That man, daintier but somehow grubbier than any of the others, knelt down beside the spilled food. He threw back his ragged sombrero, laid aside his rifle, and started picking everything up. He brushed off the cloth packets and returned them with the fruit to the hamper. Then he gathered the eggs one at a time and restored them to the wire basket. The sky brightened while he worked, and the early morning light sharpened the dirty colors of the men's serapes, revealed clearly the dusty broadcloth of the jackets on the men who didn't have wool shawls.

At last the little man in the ragged blue suit dropped the candles and box of matches into the basket. Then he picked up the suede sack.

He grunted at its weight as he reached up to hand it to the gray-haired man.

The old man rested his rifle against his thigh while he untied the bag and poured the gold pieces into his palm.

Eduardo looked at me, then at the old bandit as he asked in Spanish, "Are you men with General Villa?"

The man merely continued to stare at the handful of gold glinting in the light. He didn't look up, but finally he mused, "Ah, sí. El General," as if perhaps he had heard of Villa.

Then he sighed and poured the coins back in the bag. He looked from Matt Gordon to Eduardo, ignoring me while he harangued them in Spanish that was too rapid for me to follow. When he ran down at last, Eduardo gave a shortened translation. "He says they are part of the revolutionary army."

"With General Villa?" Matt Gordon asked.

Before Eduardo could answer, the bandit leader launched into another speech that went on for some time.

None of the other men moved or spoke, and as the sun came up, I saw that the sack of gold had vanished as completely as the stars.

When Gray Hair stopped this time, I couldn't stay quiet any longer, and I said to Eduardo, "Are they from Aguas de los Caballos?"

"He didn't tell me that, but he says they're willing to guide us to their headquarters. They're going to hitch m-mules to the truck and take us by a shortcut."

Which sounded to me as if they planned to take us by the shortest route out into the desert and abandon us. They wouldn't even have to shoot us. They could just leave us. We'd be bleached white bones within a week.

"He wants us to ride with his men, but you can stay in the truck."

"Fine."

Perhaps it would only be me they'd dump in the wilderness.

I took off my heavy blanket and folded it with what I hoped was a show of nonchalance. I'd already lost the sack of gold, but I still had the Roosevelt coins.

At least for now.

The gray-haired man with the red muffler issued orders. Some of the bandits jumped into action to fasten two tall mules to the front bumper of the Tin Lizzie, and all the men dropped their solemn demeanor to examine the Ford, guffawing and elbowing each other as they ran their hands over the fenders and rubber tires, opened and closed the metal hood. They spelled out with grimy fingers the metal script of FORD on the radiator, honked the horn, pushed and pulled the levers of the dashboard, and repeatedly tugged and released the hand brake.

They took turns raising and snapping the top half of the windshield into place until the rectangle of glass cracked.

They ignored me, and none of them seemed interested in the back compartment.

And fortunately, before one of them discovered it and decided to go through the contents, all of them except Gray Hair crowded together, hunkered down, and set about playing some kind of mumblety-peg with their knives to see who could win the right to ride in the pie wagon.

Half an hour of knife throwing went by before two of them finally triumphed and shoved their way good-naturedly away from the game to claim their prize.

The two winning bandits removed their serapes and wedged them on their saddles. Then one of them hoisted himself into the passenger seat while the other got behind the wheel. Their horses were handed off to Eduardo and Matt Gordon.

Eduardo swung easily into the saddle, but Matt Gordon had to be helped onto his horse by the bandits.

Both of them had taken off their driving dusters, and I could see that Eduardo no longer had the silver-handled pistol.

I'd figured that wouldn't do us much good.

I hadn't seen what had happened to the other plaid blankets, but I put mine on the floor and casually propped my boots on it.

Another few minutes elapsed until at last the grinning bandits seemed satisfied with their arrangements for the ride across the desert, and Gray Hair shouted, "Vamanos!"

The riders made clucking noises, flapped their reins, and jingled their stirrups. The two mules attached to the pie wagon yanked on the ropes, and the bandit in the driver's seat gleefully pretended to drive as we jerked into motion.

The bandits laughed like children on a merry-go-round when the 'driver' honked the horn and swung the steering wheel back and forth. The two mules, endeavoring to pull the pie wagon straight ahead, whinnied, flicked their ears, and arched their necks with irritation while the wheels veered right and left.

As soon as the caravan started, Gray Hair signaled, and everyone left the road beside the railroad tracks to veer off across the barren countryside.

The sun rose, and the colorless ribbons of heat reappeared.

The hooves of the mules and horses stirred up even more dirt than the Ford tires, and since the bandits cantered back and forth to watch the Tin Lizzie leaping over the uneven ground, they enclosed the truck in a barricade of human heat and dust.

As the horses and riders moved ahead, I caught occasional glimpses of Eduardo in the crowd. He did ride well, and I wouldn't have minded if he'd trotted his horse to the side of the pie wagon once or twice.

He didn't, and I clamped my lips against the grit and told myself I'd know soon enough if the bandits intended to drop me off in the wasteland.

I readjusted the ribbon of Yolanda's hat under my chin and tried not to think about that possibility or about water.

Since the bandits hadn't yet discovered the ten-quart can or the suitcases and camera equipment, I certainly didn't intend to call attention to any of them.

I closed my eyes against the sweat collecting over my eyebrows.

The bandit 'driver' wove the Tin Lizzie back and forth behind
the mules.

I lost track of how much time elapsed before I heard a shout
and opened my eyes again.

Ahead, four small adobe houses sat crumbling in the heat. I
could tell that the huts, obviously the out-buildings for a large
hacienda that had disappeared, now formed the center of a sprawl
of wagons, tents, makeshift corrals, cannons, pyramids of crates,
and a boxcar that evidently served as a barracks among the spiny
nests of yucca and thickets of cactus. A scabby row of trees mean-
dered through the camp.

Scores of men prowled around the tents and meager campfires
that spread out across the hills. As we got closer, I could see a few
women tending cooking pots, and a scattering of children chasing
each other among the tent ropes.

The bandit 'driving' the pie wagon honked the horn. Almost
everyone in the encampment dropped whatever they'd been doing
and came running out to meet us. They swarmed toward the Tin
Lizzie, and when the mules at last pulled up beside a dismantled
cannon and the largest of the adobe huts, the crowd packed around
us with suffocating heat. The men babbled among themselves in
such quick Spanish that I couldn't catch a word.

I couldn't catch a breath either, and I stood up in the back seat,
then stepped out onto the running board. I held onto the curve of
the roof and tried to swallow the dust in my mouth.

They hadn't left me in the desert at any rate.

Eduardo appeared from the crowd and climbed up beside me.

I was almost too glad to see him. "Where are we? Do you think
we're in Aguas de los Caballos?"

"I don't know."

He wiped his forehead under the brim of the sombrero and
watched while a knot of tall tanned men, clad only in loin cloths,
emerged from a nearby tent. Quivers of arrows hung across their

backs, and their long black hair dangled lank about their faces. The crowd separated for them, and when they came within a few feet of the Tin Lizzie to examine us with sharp black eyes, I caught the stench of oil used to deep-fry pork.

"Yaqui Indians," Eduardo whispered.

Papa had taken me to a traveling Wild West Show once when I was little, and I'd been saddened by the tired chiefs plodding around the ring in dirty blankets. I'd also gone to the Unique Theatre with Mama and had gotten delicious shivers from the fake savages in *Squaw Man,* but these Yaquis were nothing like those sorry performing Indians. Despite their unkempt hair and their strong odor, I'd never seen men with such physical beauty. They stood erect, holding their bows loosely and lifting their chins with pride. Their aquiline noses and strong clean jaws certainly had a better claim to aristocracy than Luther with his severe, sunburned face.

They stood looking at us in dignified silence while two bandits in grimy white cotton trousers and serapes unhitched the mules and led them away.

Just then a man sauntered from the largest of the adobe huts, and the crowd hushed into near reverence.

From my vantage point of the running board, I watched over the heads of the peasants and the Yaquis as the man progressed through the crowd. He wore a pair of khaki pants with leggings and heavy riding shoes, and in defiance of the heat, a bulky brown sweater. He also wore an English pith helmet as if he were directing a safari in Africa rather than strolling through a crowd of peasants in the middle of the Mexican desert.

He had the same kind of ruddy complexion as Luther, but he had none of Luther's stern arrogance, and he smiled with childlike friendliness below a glossy black mustache. As he stopped to speak to one of the bandits, I saw that he also had badly stained and crooked teeth.

He patted a child on the head as he walked by, moving effortlessly through the people clustered around him. Even the Yaquis
gave him their attention, and it was clear that everyone understood
he was in charge.

19

$\mathcal{A}$ FEW VOICES IN the crowd murmured "Viva, Villa," and the man beamed. He stopped a number of times to speak to people, pausing for a few minutes at the side of the gray-haired bandit/soldier who had led the way to the camp.

Then he moved on, and as he approached at a leisurely pace, the two bandits who'd ridden in the truck clambered out and snapped to attention. The Yaquis saluted.

At last he reached the pie wagon. He stopped to study it while he adjusted the British topee. He maintained a benevolent, yellow-toothed smile.

Eduardo took my hand and helped me jump down from the running board. Then he swept off his sombrero and made an extravagant bow. "Buenos días, General Villa." He straightened and extended his hand.

His theatrical bow also came off as too rehearsed even for him, and the general gazed at him a second while something flickered in his dark brown eyes.

His smile remained open and generous, but he stood absolutely still a moment before he took off the British helmet and revealed crinkly black hair that glistened with sweat. As he tucked the topee under his arm and reached for Eduardo's hand, he began a flowery speech in Spanish.

His voice echoed over the crowd, and everyone stood listening with rapt attention.

I knew he was welcoming us to his humble camp, but somehow his overblown Spanish rhetoric sounded more dramatic—and even more stagy—than Eduardo's theatrics, and although I couldn't catch all the words, I didn't believe a single one of those I could understand.

Finally the general paused and replaced the helmet over his tousled black hair.

Eduardo bowed another elaborate bow, and while he gestured at Matt Gordon, still caught in the press of the crowd, he included 'camera' and 'Hollywood' in his Spanish explanation. Then he waved his hand toward me and said, "Señorita Cooper Harrison."

General Villa—and most of the crowd—turned to stare at me.

I could feel myself blush, but I didn't see any point in lowering my gaze demurely, so I stared back at the general.

There was no way anyone would mistake him for an aristocrat.

I guessed he probably weighed around 180 pounds and stood about five feet ten, but he seemed shorter because his stocky build and the bulky sweater made him rotund. Under the rim of the helmet, his crimson face beaded with perspiration that collected to dribble from his sideburns. He had a heavy protruding jaw, and his teeth appeared even more jagged and stained than they had at a distance.

"Have we come to Aguas de los Caballos, General?" Eduardo asked in Spanish.

Villa nodded.

The little creek running beside the drying trees had to be the Waters of the Horses.

At last Eduardo finished his discourse, and I nudged him. "Can you ask if my grandfather is still here?"

General Villa gave me a semi-bow while he nodded, smiled encouragingly, and answered before Eduardo could. "Su abuelo está aquí , Señorita."

He continued to smile at me while he said something to Eduardo, who translated, "He says he would speak English to you,

but since most of his m-men do not speak it, he makes a practice
of not using it unless he is on American soil. English does not carry
the precision or the passion of Spanish, and he considers it not only
rude but vain to use in Mexico a language that does not express his
thoughts completely."

I suspected the real reason Francisco Villa didn't speak English
was that he had the same excruciatingly bad accent in it that I had
in Spanish, but of course I had no intention of suggesting that. So
I smiled and inclined my head to agree with him.

Then I fished Luther's note from my skirt pocket. "Can you ask
him—?"

Villa interrupted with a comment in Spanish.

"He says you c-can ask him yourself since he speaks English."

I'd already realized that General Villa didn't have a stutter, that
it only appeared with Eduardo's translation, and I wondered if the
general noticed as I nodded and held out the scrap of paper. "My
grandfather, mi abuelo, sent a letter from Aguas de los Caballos
saying he'd been wounded."

The general didn't glance toward the note while he murmured
something through his smile.

"He says that you may go see your grandfather yourself for a
few minutes if you wish."

"Gracias."

Villa bowed himself into another long Spanish explanation
that ended with a question aimed at me.

"He hesitates to b-bring up such matters when the señorita is
so young and has just arrived. He is doubly grieved because she is
his honored guest. But he must ask—with great reluctance—if the
señorita has brought the money her grandfather requested."

I nodded again.

"He is most unhappy to bring up the subject. He says that a
discussion of money goes against friendship and hospitality, b-but
since your grandfather desired to convince the officers of the
División del Norte that he is not a spy for Huerta or for the revo-

lutionary traitor, Carranza, Señor Harrison himself insisted on donating a substantial sum to help the troops. Your grandfather wants to prove his good will toward our brave Chihuahua soldiers, and the sooner that proof has been produced, the sooner Señor Harrison will be vindicated."

I wished I could think of a diplomatic way to explain why I no longer had the sack of gold. I watched the general's bad teeth while I hesitated.

But I couldn't come up with anything.

I took a breath. There was nothing for it but to accuse his brave Chihuahuan soldiers of stealing. "I had the ransom money for you, General Villa, when we left El Paso, but your men took it."

"Mis hombres, Señorita?"

I searched the crowd.

The gray-haired bandit leader stared directly at me, and I felt blood rushing to my head again, flaming over my face.

But there was nothing for it, and I indicated Gray Hair. "That man there seemed to be in charge." And since I'd started it, I had to keep going. "Your men took our basket of food and the sack of gold. The bag contained a collection of antique gold coins I'd prepared especially for you, General Villa."

That wasn't exactly a lie since I had dumped the coins back in the sack and I had been prepared to give them to anyone who held Luther captive.

The general gazed at me a second longer with his fixed smile before he turned and spoke to Gray Hair.

The old man produced a puzzled stare. Then he shrugged with great innocence, and began to shake his head while he murmured an extravagant denial.

A long exchange took place between Villa and the old man, then between Gray Hair and a couple of bandit/soldiers standing beside him, and finally between Villa and Eduardo, who translated, "He says that the captain did not see any gold. Neither Lieutenant

Chavez nor any of his m-men ever saw a sack of gold coins intended for the general."

After another round-robin conversation, Eduardo added, "He
says he is afraid that without the money, your grandfather's protes-
tations of good faith will have to be annulled."

I took another breath. "But I did come prepared, General, in
case I lost those particularly valuable coins." His highly embroi-
dered Spanish made me try to make my English more eloquent. "In
the event that I encountered government troops and had to give up
that sack of gold, I saved back some ransom money that—"

I broke off, turned, and stepped quickly up on the running
board of the pie wagon. I looked down at the floor.

The blanket with the Roosevelt coins had disappeared.

Adrenalin slammed into the base of my neck. My knees jellied,
and I might have tumbled off the running board if I hadn't been
holding the handrail.

Why hadn't I taken the stupid blanket when I stepped out of
the back seat?

Why hadn't I thought about it while I studied the handsome
Yaquis and listened to Eduardo translate the smiling general's
interminable speeches.

I descended shakily to the ground and looked at Villa.

"I sewed some gold coins in the hem of a blanket for safekeep-
ing in case I didn't get to Aguas de los Caballos with the sack." I gestured vaguely toward the empty space on the floor. "But it seems
that your men have taken the blanket, too."

"Lo siento, Señorita."

The general said something else to Eduardo. His smile didn't
waver, and for a brief moment, I hoped he was assuring me that he
believed me and that he'd start an immediate search for the gold.

"He's very sorry. He understands that his soldiers have an evil
reputation in your country. But he says his soldiers aren't the
thieves they're r-rumored to be by your American press."

Even though Eduardo's expression held great sympathy, I wanted to crack his beautiful head with the starter crank.

"He can guarantee that no m-man in his army would remove una cosa that belonged to him or to one of his guests. Hospitality and loyalty are sacred to him and thus to his men. He can only believe that Señor Harrison never intended to pay."

"My grandfather had every intention of paying! The loss of the money was my fault!"

Villa opened his mouth, but I raised my voice over what he might have said, "I did bring a sack of gold, and I did sew a thousand American dollars into the hem of a blanket in case I ran into the federales!" I took a jagged breath. "On my grandfather's instructions, I brought you the ransom."

Villa made a brief statement.

"He says 'ransom' is an ugly word. He says your grandfather volunteered freely to help the rebellion. There was never a question of coercion. Señor Harrison said he wished to convince the revolutionary soldiers of his loyalty, but apparently he never intended to hand over the m-money. All along he obviously considered the men of the División del Norte ignorant peasants who could be easily fooled."

Villa smiled from Eduardo to me. "Lo siento."

"He is sorry, b-but it seems inevitable now that your grandfather will be shot at sunset."

20

THE ADOBE HUTS beyond the crowd tilted, and I propped my shoulder against the sun-baked side of the pie wagon. I was sure my temples pounded loud enough under Yolanda's hat to echo across the cactus plain.

I couldn't remember a worse moment.

Not even the terrible afternoon Rosalie told me my parents had died. That awful day I'd been comforted by the knowledge that the doctors, Papa's parishioners—everyone—had done all that could be done against the epidemic. Nothing had been left up to me, and no one expected me to do anything.

But now, it was all left up to me.

And I'd botched it.

Through my own thoughtlessness.

I leaned against the hot gilt script, HARRISON AND ROBARTS ANTIQUES, on the wooden compartment.

Eduardo took a step toward me, but to forestall him, I forced myself away from the side of the truck. And to avoid brushing him off, I pretended I hadn't noticed he'd been about to offer me his arm. I said to Villa, "You told me I could see my grandfather."

"For a few minutes. I would not d-deny you the chance to say good-bye, Señorita."

General Villa spoke to a bandit who wore puttees over sandals and a too-tight pin-striped vest with a gray worsted jacket. Not a button remained on the jacket, but neither it nor the vest spanned the man's chest anyway, and they gaped open on a silk shirt that was too filthy to have any color. The cuffs of both the shirt and the jacket had raveled to spidery threads.

The bandit, who wore a gold signet ring on his middle finger and who held his rifle like a walking stick, nodded, smiled happily beneath his black mustache, and beckoned to me. I had no alternative but to plunge after him into the solemn staring crowd.

The Yaqui Indians, the peasant soldiers, the women and children parted for the bandit and me, and I could feel their eyes boring into me. My face ran with sweat, but I walked with my head up and didn't look at anyone even though I felt occasional fingers reaching out to touch the material of my skirt and sash.

Dust grayed my boots before I'd taken more than a few steps, but I followed the bandit through the gaping crush of peasants until we finally emerged. The rebel in the ridiculous leather leggings that left his dirty toes exposed continued along a footpath until we came to a hut guarded by two more bandit/soldiers wearing filthy white cottons.

This temporary hut had been hammered together from rough boards, but it sat beside a sturdy eight-foot adobe wall that had probably once bordered an orchard. The sloughing stucco of the wall now stood pocked with bullet holes and stained with rust, and clusters of spear-leaved yucca had replaced anything that might have grown in a garden.

My grinning guide chatted cheerfully with the two guards, who nodded and beamed around their black mustaches, but I didn't catch enough words to identify the topic. They enjoyed themselves for a few minutes until at last the bandit stepped toward me in his sandals and puttees, patted my arm, and issued some smiling instructions.

I didn't understand them either, but since one of the other bandits unlocked a padlock and lifted a metal bar from across the make-shift door, I assumed the three of them had agreed to let me go inside. I also assumed that Luther would be there.

The guard pulled open the shoddy slats, which had the look of a door confiscated from a ramshackle barn, and gestured. "Vaya, Señorita."

I ducked in.

The little hut had no windows, and when the man shut the door behind me, suffocating black heat enveloped me.

It was déjà vu.

I might have been entering Luther's shuttered house again for the first time.

"Yolanda?" Luther's voice came from across the darkness.

I peered toward the sound, but I couldn't see a thing. "It's Cooper," I said. "I'm wearing Yolanda's hat."

"Stay where you are."

I'd been with him for less than a heartbeat, and he'd already barked an order.

"There are only chinks of light. It'll take a minute."

Since he was right and my eyes hadn't adjusted to the gloom, I didn't argue. I merely took off Yolanda's hat and waited until gradually I could make out vague shapes in the semi-illumination.

A broad-shouldered man sat on a pallet against one wall, and in the opposite corner stood the dim outline of a pail. A gully cut across the dirt floor as if the hut had been built over a dry riverbed.

"Don't move. I'll come to you."

That didn't seem worth arguing about either, so I stood still while he got up from the mattress and crossed the ditch toward me.

He no longer wore his suit jacket or vest, and he no longer had either shoes or socks. I'd probably seen his slouch hat on one of the bandits in the camp, and I didn't have to ask if he still had his gold watch.

His right shirt-sleeve had been rolled above a thick bandage that covered his arm to the elbow.

"Is that the wound you mentioned? Is it your arm?"

"Never mind. How did you get here? Did you bring the money?"

He stopped close beside me so we could whisper, and I was struck again by the fact that we stood the same height. I answered to his second question first. "I started from El Paso with the gold. But Villa's men took it before I could turn it over to the general himself."

"Villa didn't get the ransom money?"

I floundered for a kinder word than 'bandit' in case the guards had their ears pressed against the door slats and in case they understood English. "The soldiers discovered the coins right away."

He nodded.

"I was afraid that might happen, though, so I brought the five-dollar Roosevelt coins as well. I sewed them in the hem of a blanket so I could keep it beside me."

"And—?"

"I got here with it. But it was also stolen before I could give it to General Villa."

His broad shoulders slumped.

"Why does he think you're a spy anyway?"

"He's suspicious of everyone. He wanders around the camp eating a meal with a different soldier every night so no one will know whose food he'll sample and no one will be able to poison him. He's particularly suspicious of Americans."

"But why does he think you're a spy now?" I persisted. "You certainly haven't tried to poison him, and you've been smuggling bullets to him. Doesn't that mean you've been on his side all this time?"

"Huerta's men attacked a patrol of Villa's while I was still on the road. They blew up a bridge, and the wagon and my supplies got caught in the crossfire. Huerta's troops found the bullets and were distributing the sacks of corn when Villa's men counter-attacked. It appeared that I'd gone over to the government forces. I insisted I'd been bringing the ammunition to Villa himself, and I offered to make good on the bullets Huerta's men made off with. But with all the gold gone now—"

"Well, we do have one more—" I brought myself up short.

If the bandit/soldiers at the door could decipher my whisper, the diamonds would be gone before I set foot outside. So I said instead, "What happened to Tomás?"

"Villa's men gave him the choice of joining the División del Norte or of being executed on the spot. He made the only logical decision and joined the rebels."

"They didn't give you the same choice?"

"I'm an American."

"That's what I mean. Isn't that a good thing? Won't that work in your favor?" The sunlight shifted, and in a narrow band beamed through a splintered board, I could see his unshaven jaw glinting with silver bristles. "Villa hasn't executed any Americans."

"There's always a first time."

"General Pershing said Villa wants to keep Wilson's good will by not appropriating American haciendas or companies. Won't shooting you cause more mischief than it's worth?"

Luther shrugged.

"General Villa knows that if he executes you, Americans will turn against the revolution, doesn't he?"

"Most Americans don't care a straw about the revolution."

"Some of them do. Those Hollywood people have been following it closely. They're the main reason I got here. I drove into Mexico in your pie wagon with them. They're making that film of Villa's life, so he's all smiles around them. I think they may be able to influence him to let you out of here."

"I wouldn't put too much stock in Pancho Villa's smiles or his good will if I were you or those Hollywood people. Jack Pershing says Villa is at his most dangerous when he's smiling. And, of course, he's always smiling."

That was true. He'd even smiled while he expressed regret about shooting Luther.

"But I still don't see how he can go through with executing you."

"If he does, you'll have to take care of the business and your grandmother."

He'd obviously come to terms with the fact that he wasn't going back to El Paso with me.

In the little shaft of light, he looked frazzled and seedy in his bare feet and suit trousers, with his soiled shirt that had lost its celluloid collar, and the filthy bandage on his arm. He watched me with a bleak expression

"Angelica needs someone to take care of her. There's no one left but you."

I gave a sort of a shake/nod of my head to indicate that I could take care of her even though I wasn't thoroughly convinced that she needed as much help as either of them thought.

The light altered, shone directly into my eyes, and I put on Yolanda's hat again.

In spite of the possible listeners at the door, I had to reveal that last hope of ransom to him.

I leaned closer.

But before I could whisper that I'd also brought some diamonds, he added hoarsely, "And if anything happens to me, I want you to promise me you'll take care of Yolanda's baby."

"Yolanda's baby?" I straightened.

Suddenly I understood.

Everything.

In my shock, I recoiled from him and backed into the door.

Which at that moment was flung open by the bandit/soldier in the silk shirt, who grabbed my arm. "Venga, Señorita."

21

I LET MYSELF BE dragged outside before I glared back at Luther.

Just as the guard slammed the door and dropped the iron bar across it, I realized that the bandage on Luther's arm stopped short of his hand.

That realization thudded into the other revelation with such unexpectedness that dizziness swept over me.

Luther had lost his hand in the battle near Aguas de los Caballos.

Luther was the father of Yolanda's baby.

Those realities careened around my skull as I turned to walk numbly beside the rebel soldier who finally dropped his gold-ringed hand from my arm.

We passed a mound of cactus, and when the needles danced in the harsh light, I almost staggered. I could feel the bandit glance at me, but I didn't look at him as I steadied myself and kept walking.

I had no idea where he was taking me, but I didn't ask.

I couldn't have. I couldn't have uttered a coherent syllable at that moment—in either English or Spanish—if Luther's life, Eduardo's, and my own depended on it.

So I'd guessed wrong. Yolanda hadn't been blackmailing Luther after all. He'd been giving her gifts because she was having his baby.

What else had I guessed wrong about?

No wonder she lashed out so defensively when I said I considered him old.

We passed another wild, dusty tumble of cactus pads. Pale yellow flowers bloomed in single file along the curved rims, and the spines spun off barbs of frenzied light.

Yolanda wore expensive gold earrings that came from Luther. And at the moment, she was probably wearing Mama's black straw hat.

I abruptly wanted to race back to the little hut and yell at my grandfather.

I wanted to charge him with betraying everything I needed him to stand for. Of betraying Angelica. Of dishonoring Papa's memory by being worse than Keith Boudreaux.

But of course he didn't even know who Keith Boudreaux was.

And of course I couldn't turn and run anyway. Every man jack in the encampment had a rifle, and I'd make too easy a target.

So I managed to walk quietly beside the dirty peasant through the dirty square.

No one loitered any longer beside the adobe walls or hung around the pie wagon. An eerie stillness surrounded the empty area. The Yaquis, Villa's rag-tag soldiers, and all the camp followers had retired to their tents and boxcar quarters beside the little stream. And although I could see beyond the trees campfire smoke and dust stirred up by the horses, I couldn't hear anything but the slap of the soldier's sandals against the dirt.

I swallowed another urge to scream out an accusation at Luther that would carry to the prison hut. He'd acted more shabbily than anyone I'd ever known.

The soldier and I passed the pie wagon. The doors to the back were closed, and I told myself that if the diamonds had already disappeared, I couldn't be expected to rescue Luther. I had done what I could, and if the last glittering rocks of his ransom had been stolen, he'd have to take his chance with the firing squad.

He was the father of Yolanda's baby.

And the saddest thing was that I'd actually begun to like him.

The silk-shirted bandit and I reached the largest adobe hut. "Señorita."

The door stood open, and I could see white stucco walls inside.

"Aquí," he repeated louder to make certain I understood. "La casa del General Villa." He made a grimy hand movement that resembled a farewell wave more than it did a beckon, but he repeated "Venga," as he went through the open door.

I followed him into a room that was surprisingly cool.

Two peasant soldiers in pieced-together outfits, shabby sombreros, and glossy black mustaches stood watch with their rifles cocked and ready. They eyed me warily as my guide led me across the hard-swept dirt floor to a closed door guarded by two more men with cautious eyes, rifles, and ammunition belts.

"La Señorita está aquí," the bandit said, and one of guards knocked.

When a "Sí" came from inside, the guard opened the door and said, "La Señorita, mi General."

They let me walk into the room alone.

General Villa stood behind a battered desk, and Matt Gordon and Eduardo stood nonchalantly before him on a threadbare carpet spread over the dirt floor. Two little girls, dressed in identical dimity gowns, sat together on a mohair sofa at one side of the room. My quick glance at them showed that even though one child had brown hair and one had curly black hair, they were both daughters of Pancho Villa.

As I stepped onto the worn rug that I could tell had once been expensive, Villa bowed and snapped his fingers toward the peasant at the door. "Un otro jugo de naranja!"

"Sí, mi General." The man pulled the door shut.

As my brain registered that Eduardo and Matt Gordon and the two little girls held glasses of orange juice, my peripheral vision recorded suitcases, the camera, and boxes of equipment. I was almost certain the water can and dipper sat among the canisters of film, but I didn't look toward them to make sure. I looked steadily at Villa.

He no longer wore the khaki pants and baggy brown sweater but had changed to a resplendent white uniform topped with gold epaulettes and a collar encrusted with gold braid. Dozens of gold and silver medals hung from the multi-colored ribbons pinned on the front of the jacket, and as he bowed to me the medals swung and glittered.

He looked ridiculous, and despite his black mustache, in the split second before he smiled and spoke to Eduardo, he bore an uncanny resemblance to Luther.

"The general hopes you found your grandfather in g-good health."

Eduardo suddenly sounded very young. Had his stutter gotten worse?

But I tried to concentrate on Villa. "My grandfather lost his hand."

I hadn't meant to say that, and I amended quickly with, "Tell the general I want to thank him for having someone bandage my grandfather's wrist stump."

That wasn't right either. I was supposed to talk directly to Villa, not use Eduardo as a go-between.

Villa didn't correct me this time, however, and Eduardo translated, "The general says he had his personal doctor take c-care of your grandfather. But it would be better for a hospital to treat Señor Harrison's arm soon."

"Yes, I—"

"Que lástima —" Villa interrupted.

"—that the Señorita has nothing left to give as a monetary recompense."

I took a breath. I had prepared one more monetary recompense. I took a breath.

No matter how I felt about Luther, I had to give him a last chance, so I said as loud as I could, "Can I be certain you'll release my grandfather if I pay, General?"

I knew I was taking a chance as a female, and as a foreigner, but nonetheless I let myself question his honesty. And I asked as loud as I could.

The two little girls tensed, and Eduardo gaped at my audacity, but for a brief second, I felt much better.

Raising my voice to Villa had almost been as satisfying as shouting at Luther.

I expected Villa to drop the smile instantly.

But he didn't. Instead an expression of approval crossed his face. "I like your straightforwardness, Señorita. I no doubt have an evil reputation in your country. But you m-must believe that I am a trustworthy man."

"I want your word that my grandfather can leave for El Paso if I'm able to fulfill his pledge."

"Por supuesto." He nodded cherrily, and Eduardo didn't need to translate.

A knock came on the door, and this time a different soldier than my silk-shirted bandit came in with a tumbler of orange juice. I couldn't help wondering if it had been squeezed from the oranges Yolanda packed the day before.

The soldier leaned across the desk and spoke softly as he gave the glass to Villa.

He obviously delivered bad news because, for the first time, the smile did vanish from General Villa's full lips. His eyes lost their benevolence, and in the space of a second, his face contorted with rage.

Finally, as if he couldn't stand to hear any more, he gave the soldier a violent shove. Orange juice splashed out onto the desk papers, and Villa clenched his stained teeth as he came around the desk, pushed the soldier toward the door, and held out the glass to me. "Señorita."

I took the juice while the soldier slunk away, and Villa lashed out in a passionate speech.

Saliva sprayed from his lips and anger shot from his narrowed eyes as he beckoned the little girls, then stormed out with them and slammed the door. His heavy stride reminded me of Luther.

We looked after them a second before Matt Gordon said, "What was all that about, Ed?"

"Word just came from Chihuahua City that President Wilson plans to lift the arms embargo for Venustino Carranza. But he intends to keep it in place for Villa."

"I thought Villa was America's most popular revolutionary. I thought that was why we come here in the first place."

"I think Villa's popularity is declining in Washington. General Obregon sided with Carranza and since he now holds Mexico City, it looks like Carranza may be the h-horse the American government has decided to back."

There were too many players in the revolution, and since my head ached, I quit trying to sort out the names and took a swallow of orange juice.

"You suppose this'll make the filming harder, Ed? After we lugged all them boxes a candy half way across the country."

Eduardo glanced at me. "The general doesn't drink or smoke, but his men say he'd rather have candy than guns."

A box of chocolates in place of sacks of bullets and corn would certainly have saved Luther time and effort—and maybe his hand.

"We brought a separate crate for the uniform, too," Matt Gordon moaned.

I'd wondered where Villa had found such a gaudy outfit.

"It's supposed to make him stand out in the film."

I thought Villa would stand out much better in his brown outfit and English helmet, but I didn't say it.

Nor did I get a chance to say anything else as General Villa thundered into the room again and blazed out in another tirade.

"Your country has betrayed me. Your schemers and traitors

146

surround me, and your president is siding with the Creole Carranza." He gathered up juice-spattered papers and stuffed them into a dusty saddlebag. "Carranza has white, very white skin, but I am to your president a dark-complexioned and ignorant p-peasant." Villa turned to glare at me in particular. "Your grandfather is a spy, a p-pawn of your government."

"He's not a spy, General!"

"His execution will show how we deal with those who betray us."

"He hasn't betrayed you! I came to fulfill his pledge. If you will just—"

"Your president, who meddles in other's politics, has c-condemned him. He will be executed at once."

"It's not fair to hold my grandfather responsible for what President Wilson does. He doesn't even like Wilson."

"Your president would p-prefer that Carranza rule Mexico. Venustino Carranza behaves properly and drinks tea with his pinkie extended. He is pale skinned and respectable, and your president will welcome him to Washington as the ruler of Mexico's little brown brothers."

Villa stuffed the last of the papers into the saddlebag and scowled at Matt Gordon. "There are government soldiers, Huerta's men, camped in the Valle de Cauca, and my m-men, mis hermanos de la raza, who do not care if I am a Mexican peasant, will attack within the hour. I keep my promises. You can film your battle in the daylight."

"You asked for—" Now I wanted to be diplomatic, but my scuttled brain couldn't find a substitute word that wouldn't agitate him. "You asked for ransom, and I brought it, General Villa."

"It is too late. I shall dispose of Señor Harrison before we attack Huerta's men."

"My grandfather has been your friend. He behaved honorably to you."

I hoped that was true.

"You are either very brave or very impolitic, Señorita."

I blundered on quickly, "My grandfather and General Pershing are also good friends. It would be a shame to tell the American general that you executed a man who was close to you both."

The unexpected approval crossed Villa's ruddy face again.

"You m-may be impertinent, but you speak courageously, Señorita."

His face cleared and he motioned to Eduardo. "For the sake of the señorita, I will let her grandfather live until we return. You may go visit him one more time, Señorita."

"I don't know if I want to see him again!"

I felt Eduardo gape at me, but I watched Villa's stained teeth flash into a smile.

"But I must warn you not to expect leniency, Señorita. I shall bring the firing squad b-back with me from the field, and your grandfather will be shot."

22

$\mathcal{T}$HE GENERAL strode out again.

Matt Gordon and Eduardo located their hats and began sorting through the equipment piled around the room.

Matt Gordon took the lid off the water can and filled the dipper.

Before they could decide to take the can, I said quickly, "My grandfather needs the water if that's all right with you."

"That's f-fine."

Eduardo took a drink and handed me the dipper. As I rescued the can, I saw that about a third of the water was left. Maybe the diamonds still rolled around inside.

"Since you're a guest of the general, you'll be all r-right alone here until we return."

"Of course I'll be all right." My voice sharpened. "You're the one who needs to be careful!"

"He ain't fighting," Matt Gordon said. "Being behind a camera ain't the same as being behind a rifle. Ed's mother'd never forgive me if I let him flounder into a battle."

Eduardo blushed. "I thought I was supposed to protect you."

Before Matt Gordon could respond, a peasant/soldier guard reappeared and herded us all outside.

Matt Gordon and Eduardo carried equipment, and I clung tight to the water can.

Shouting and bustling had returned to the street, and while the bandits helped load the camera and boxes into a wagon, a troop on horseback cantered by.

Through the dust, I saw Francisco Villa riding stiff legged on a great black horse. He'd added an officer's cap with more gold braid across the bill to the white uniform that blazed with medals and ribbons, and he looked even more ludicrous than he had before.

But despite his obvious discomfort, he smiled as he rode past.

He didn't look toward Eduardo or Matt Gordon as the two of them climbed into the wagon bed and the soldier on the box snapped the mules into motion.

Eduardo waved as they disappeared into the dust behind Villa's cavalry.

More peasants rode by, followed by an ambulance cart, a cannon on a two-wheeled cart, and two more wagons.

On the box of the second wagon, Tomás, dressed in the peasant once-white cotton outfit and a wide-brimmed sombrero, cracked his whip in the air above the mottled brown and white back of a familiar horse.

At least they'd been able to stay together. At least Tomás would be able to say, "Whoa, Raphael," whenever he felt like it.

Neither of them looked toward me standing beside the adobe hut, and I didn't dare call out to them.

Now that I'd determined to give Luther his one last chance, I couldn't afford for anyone to notice me. So I clutched the handle of the can and looked wistfully after Tomás and the mottled horse.

It occurred to me that I might never see either of them again.

I watched as they, too, disappeared into the billowing dust.

I stood motionless and waited until a company of foot soldiers ambled across the square, accompanied by another cannon pulled by four mules. The Yaquis passed with their bows and arrows, but now they also shouldered rifles, and they'd added the omnipresent bandoliers of bullets across their naked chests. They were followed by a group of women, some in cotton pants and shirts, some in skirts and blouses with cockades in their hats. They, too, walked barefoot, carried rifles and ammunition belts, and a few cradled babies across their breasts.

The babies gazed from the blanket slings with solemn dark eyes.

Luther requested that in case of his execution I should be responsible for Yolanda's baby.

And I realized that no matter how I felt about Luther, I wasn't indecisive about the baby. Of course I'd take care of it. It would be my aunt or uncle. It would be my blood relative as much as it would be Yolanda's, and it might even look like me or Papa.

I watched a line of children, laden down with extra cartridge belts, straggle after the women. Dirt mixed the air into the thick syrupiness of café con leche and the cloud followed the troop into the desert.

I stood a long time while the riders and walkers disappeared behind the column of tan dust.

At last the street emptied.

I waited another few minutes, preparing myself to see Luther again, before I left the narrow strip of shade, passed the Tin Lizzie, and walked as calmly as I could to the tiny prison.

I noticed again the wall behind the hut, and I abruptly realized that the stain wasn't rust but dried blood. It would be where Villa would stand Luther for his execution if it came to that.

I looked away and saw the two guards watching me approach, "General Villa told me to bring my grandfather some water."

They stared at me a long moment, trying to decipher my badly accented Spanish.

They may not have understood the lie, but since I stood firm, waiting, finally one of them unlocked the padlock and lifted the metal bar.

"Luther," I shouted into the hut. My voice wavered, but I nonetheless told the lie again. "General Villa told me to bring you some water. He gave me permission to visit you a last time. He's gone to attack the federales."

I went inside. The door shut, and I stood, letting my pupils adjust while Luther got up from the pallet to join me.

"That was thoughtful of the general."

"Yes." I set the can down on the dirt floor, took off the lid, and filled the dipper for him.

I watched him drink greedily.

When he finished and handed me back the dipper, I rolled up my sleeve, knelt down, and plunged my arm into the water. I ran my hand around the can.

Had someone found the diamonds after all?

Then my fingers encountered a small hard object on the floor of the can.

The object slipped away, but I managed to catch it, and when I withdrew my arm from the water, I held the dripping square-cut facets tight in my fist.

I stood up again and opened my palm.

An emerald-cut diamond of perhaps three karats lay in my wet hand.

"Ah." Luther gazed down with admiration. He dropped into a whisper again. "They are beautiful, aren't they?"

"I suppose," I whispered coldly. "If you like ice chips."

"You sound just like Alex."

I dropped the diamond into his palm. "Do you think this will ransom you?"

"Are there others?"

I nodded. "I might need some bargaining room."

"How many?"

"Five more."

"You brought six? How big?"

"About that size."

He looked silently at the large diamond before he said, "Angelica was the most beautiful creature I ever laid eyes on. I wanted to protect her, to shower her with diamonds." He turned his hand for the thread of light to hit the stone. "But I suppose women with great beauty always have a difficult time."

I waited.

Finally he looked up. "You've met Villa. How many stones do you think he'll be satisfied with? If you save some of the stones back, we can—"

I stared at him a moment before I comprehended what he was getting at. "You're actually considering risking your life to protect your stolen loot?"

"I was thinking of Angelica and Yolanda—" He broke off. "Besides, these diamonds weren't stolen. I purchased them from the best diamond merchants."

"Don't quibble. You purchased them with money from other stolen goods. It's the same thing."

He stared down at the diamond. "You don't understand. You see, El Paso is like another country. It's as foreign as Mexico. Here on the border, in both countries, there's a—" He hesitated. "—a practice known as the 'casa chica,' 'the little house.'"

"Why don't we decide what to do about your ransom before we go into a language lesson," I said.

He ignored that. "When it's time for girls on the border to marry, there often aren't enough men to go around. They've been killed one way or another. In bandit shoot-outs or in revolutions like the ones happening now. So married men sometimes choose to have another family with a young woman."

I glowered. "Yolanda's not a young woman. She's a child! She can't even read!"

He ignored that, too. "The first wife keeps the large house, and the second family stays in the little house. It's an arrangement many Texans and Mexicans make. The wives accept it as part of the way of life here on the border."

"Bigamy is illegal!"

"It's not bigamy."

"Adultery is every bit as ugly!"

"It's not adultery either. It's an arrangement. As long as a wife has respect and love in her own house, she doesn't care about the casa chica."

I walked away from him and the little spot of light.

Everything about him and Angelica and all the reasons his son had stayed away from them became blindingly clear.

"It's not an 'arrangement' I'd ever accept," I said.

"I know."

I took a breath, came back into the light, and held out my hand for the diamond.

He gave it to me. "How many are you going to offer Villa?"

I dropped the diamond into the water can.

It made a gentle splash, and I clapped on the lid.

"I'll decide when General Villa gets back from his battle," I said coldly. Then I raised my voice toward the guards outside, "Let me out! I'm ready to leave now!"

23

I DIDN'T WANT to think about Luther or his lame explanation of the 'casa chica,' but when I went back to the adobe house—which no longer had a guard at any door—and sank down on the couch where Villa's little girls had sat, Luther and Yolanda and Angelica were all I could think about.

I set the water can at the side of the sofa near my dusty boots. I wasn't about to let this ransom payment out of my sight or out of my reach.

The cut-out square of adobe behind the desk had no glass, and the faint breath of a breeze came through.

Of course, I'd never heard of such a thing as a casa chica. But then—just as Luther had said—El Paso was like a foreign country.

But foreign or not, and no matter how scant the supply of men on the border and in Mexico might be, the whole idea of a second family in a second tiny house repelled me.

I took off Yolanda's hat and laid it beside me on the mohair couch.

Naturally, Papa would have rejected the casa chica idea out of hand.

Then I re-heard Luther saying I sounded just like Alex.

At the same moment, I heard the overlap of Mama laughing good-humoredly at Papa and me.

"You and Cooper are just alike," she'd often derided. "Don't be so judgmental," I could hear her saying. In this instance she might

have added, "If this casa chica thing is an arrangement that everyone on the border understands and accepts, who are you to con-
demn it? What do you really know about other people's relation-
ships? What does something like this matter if no one gets hurt?
Muslims allow men to have many wives as long as they can afford
to support them and the children. And when the Mormons have a
shortage of men, a man can have more than one wife."

Mama knew things like that. She also had a way of dragging her
information into conversations when—as she put it—Papa and I
got too full of ourselves.

I leaned back against the rough mohair of the couch and closed
my eyes.

"If I were you two, I wouldn't throw stones at any plate glass
windows just yet," Mama would have laughed.

She would also have crocheted a doily for the back of the sofa
so people with sweat- or pomade-slick hair wouldn't ruin the
upholstery.

Luther said Angelica understood the arrangement. So who was
I to object on her behalf?

I opened my eyes and stared at the stucco ceiling.

Just as Mama would have said, I didn't know much about their
relationship.

Or about his relationship with Yolanda.

At any rate, he hadn't betrayed me.

The adobe rooms had become very still, and I heard a clock
ticking somewhere.

I listened a few seconds before I closed my eyes again.

It didn't matter what time it was.

There wasn't anything I could do until General Francisco Villa
returned from his daytime battle that promised Matt Gordon a
chance to film the shooting and killing in sunlight.

I adjusted my back and stretched my boots out on the shabby
carpet. I rested my ankle against the water can while I kept my eyes
closed.

I was thinking new thoughts now. Perhaps Mama had been
right. I had been too judgmental. Besides, when Yolanda had her
baby, Angelica and Luther wouldn't be the only two people on the
planet related to me. I'd have a little aunt or uncle. A little boy or
girl who'd be part of my family.

Somewhere beyond my eyelids, I heard children's voices, and I
dragged my eyes open.

The two little girls I'd seen before stood in the middle of the
carpet looking at me.

Of course General Villa would have children by more than one
woman. Naturally, in the accepted way of life along the Rio Grande,
a man of his stature, a man of his ripe old age of thirty-six, would
have two or more wives, two or more casas chicas. Villa was just like
Luther.

The little girls saw my eyes open and giggled. Then they began
to chatter at me in shrill child voices, and I smiled at them even as
I didn't catch half of what they said.

I sat up, and when my head swam, I realized I hadn't had anything but that glass of orange juice the entire day.

I wanted to ask the little girls if they could find me a dry crust
of bread somewhere.

But since I didn't know if asking for something to eat might be
a breach of hospitality, might incense Pancho Villa when he
returned, I didn't interrupt their babble for a long time.

They didn't seem to run out of things to say, however, and
finally I broke in with, "Qué hora es, niñas?"

They rattled on, but I knew they'd understood when the brown
haired one held up eight little fingers.

It was past eight o'clock!

"Verdad?"

They both nodded.

How long had the troops been gone?

Surely the battle had been decided by now.

But if so, how had it come out?

How long ago had the mules pulled the pie wagon into Aguas de los Caballos?

I wished I'd noticed what time in the morning that had been.

I didn't know how many of Huerta's government men Villa had gone to attack or how many men he'd taken with him.

I could at least have noticed how large a troop had filed by in the dust.

Would General Villa be in a furious mood from a defeat? Or would he be appeased by a victory?

Of course he might have Luther shot either way—in pique or in celebration.

The little girls scooted Yolanda's hat out of the way and climbed onto the sofa beside me. They each pulled a length of string from their dress pockets and began making cat's cradles.

Each time they finished a design, they showed me, and I smiled and nodded before they laughed happily, unraveled the strings, and started over.

The light in the room faded, and the furniture around us darkened.

As I continued to respond to the children, my lips began to ache from the smiles.

How could Villa keep smiling so constantly?

The little fingers wove the strings, but since the sun had gone down now, I had to look more closely to see the intricate twists and loops.

The room had become almost totally dark before hooves, voices, shouts, and spurts of laughter came from outside.

Then the door to the room banged open, and General Villa, followed by a number of men jostled into the room, talking in loud exclamations. Half a dozen of them carried candles in hurricane lanterns, and I wondered if the candles were those Yolanda had packed. The general's white uniform with the medals on the jacket glittered in the light.

"Niñas," General Villa cried as he spied the little girls.

They scrambled down from the couch, rushed to him, and clasped him about the knees.

Two women, who had followed the crowd of men through the door, edged around the soldiers to watch the children. One woman had brown hair, the other had long black locks that hung over her shoulders, Indian straight.

Villa knelt down and I guessed he was asking the children why they were up so late. But he and the women smiled, and I could tell he was pleased to have the little girls in the room to greet him.

Finally, he stood and sent the girls scurrying away with their two mothers before he greeted me with a gallant bow. "Señorita."

Despite the flickering light, I could tell his smile was more genuine, his mood much improved. And when he dropped the officer's cap on the desk, ran his hand over his black hair, and gave a series of cheerful orders to the men waiting around him, I guessed that the battle had gone well for him.

Finally the men saluted and filed out, and the general and I were left alone in the room.

I sat forward on the sofa. "Dónde están Eduardo Jimenez y Matt Gordon?"

"Sus amigos? Where?" He repeated the last word in English before he answered me in Spanish.

But I didn't know enough words to follow his explanation. The only one I understood immediately was 'muerto.'

I threw myself off the sofa and stood up so suddenly that blood rushed from my head. "They're dead?"

"No, no. Ambos, no, no." He shook his head.

Then he signed, exhibiting two fingers and bent one down, while he told me in slower Spanish what had happened.

My temples throbbed in the candlelight that flickered around the room.

He extended his forefinger and thumb while he folded his other fingers over his palm. He put the finger to his temple, mimed a shot, and closed his eyes to indicate falling over dead. Then he

repeated the primitive sign language of subtraction again, showing
me two fingers then one.

It was obvious that only one of them had been killed.

"Who?" I raised my voice. "Which of mis amigos está muerto?"

He looked at me with his unchanging smile.

I stood there dizzy with hunger and panic until at last he went
to the door and opened it. He motioned to someone in the first
room. "Venga."

24

$\mathcal{E}$DUARDO WALKED IN.

He carried Matt Gordon's gray fedora.

I could have hugged him with relief, but when Villa threw an arm around his shoulder, I stayed where I was.

Eduardo no longer wore his sombrero, and he somehow seemed younger and paler than when he'd gone off with the troops and the general.

General Villa murmured and patted him on the arm, and although he still smiled, it was a kind smile that obviously tried to console Eduardo.

But sorrow had sharpened all of his handsome features and he averted his eyes from the general and me.

We stood in awkward silence until he said at last in a choked voice, "M-Matt's dead."

I saw tears glisten in his eyes, and I waited while General Villa repeated a few low words.

Eduardo wiped a cheek with his free hand. "Sí, yo sé," he said before he turned to me. "We'd finished filming. We were packing up the camera when he got hit."

He swallowed and wiped his other cheek. "Matt filmed the entire battle without any. . . ." He groped for a word. ". . .without any m-mishap. And then when we were folding up the camera, a stray bullet got him in the back." He choked again, but swallowed. "He

didn't even groan. The bullet went through his spine and straight
into his heart. I was supposed to watch out for him."

He rubbed his hand again over his forehead and cheekbones.

General Villa watched him a long moment before his full smile
returned. He picked up one of the lanterns and went to the door.
"Comida," he explained to me over his shoulder while he made a
spooning motion with one hand.

As he went into the hallway, Eduardo said, "He's ordering dinner."

"Yes, I got that. I also gather he won the battle?"

Eduardo nodded. "Matt caught the entire thing on film. Horses
and men and dust and gunpowder and—Villa executed the officers
and foot soldiers who refused to join his troops. But then after it
was all over—"

He went to the desk, then to the square in the wall without
glass, and stood with his back to me looking out at the night. I
heard him murmur, "What am I going to tell Mother?"

General Villa came back in the room and watched him.

I took a breath.

"General, I have one other payment for my grandfather."

He didn't say anything, perhaps from sympathy so Eduardo
wouldn't have to translate.

"I only want your word, your handshake, that you will let me
take my grandfather back to El Paso."

He merely stood watching me, smiling and waiting.

It didn't matter if he gave me his word or not. I'd have to trust
him now.

I went to the water can and removed the lid. I knelt on the carpet beside the can, and the hard-packed floor was like stone
beneath the threadbare weave. I dipped into the remaining water
and felt around for the diamonds.

Finding the stones was easier this time, and I withdrew them
one at a time and put them dripping in my other hand.

I hadn't noticed particularly when I'd dropped them in the can, but now I saw I'd grabbed diamonds in various cuts, square, round, and oval. I also knew that Luther had picked them all for brilliance of sparkle and clarity.

Eduardo glanced once over his shoulder, but no one said anything.

At last I'd rescued all six diamonds, and I got up from my knees again.

I went to the general and held out my palm. "My grandfather understands diamonds," I said. "He bought only the best."

The wet diamonds glittered more fiercely in the candle flames than they had even in the daylight of Luther's shop.

"Claro," he said.

Eduardo didn't turn from the window, but Pancho Villa didn't need a translator now. He held out his hand, and I poured a large part of Luther's fortune into it.

General Villa turned his palm back and forth to let the sparkle of the facets career around the room.

I stood before him with my own hand outstretched. "I ask for your handshake on the bargain, General."

He murmured something, and Eduardo said without turning from the window, "I don't let anyone dictate to m-me, Señorita."

"I'm not dictating, General Villa. When my grandfather wrote to me, he said you would let him go if I came with the money he promised. A bargain is a bargain."

General Villa looked up from the half dozen stones in his hand to me and smiled. His teeth were pure gold in the candlelight.

"Bueno," he said. "Me gusta su espíritu, Señorita." Eduardo repeated in English, "I like your spirit."

Villa poured the diamonds into his left hand and gave me his right.

His fingers were larger than mine and very warm as he gripped my hand.

"We can start tomorrow?" I said.

He studied me a long moment, holding the smile. Then he nodded.

In the flurry of the next few minutes, he called in guards, the black-haired woman, and I was shown to a room with a simple bed and bureau. Then the brown haired woman brought me a glass of goat's milk, a little basket with warm tortillas, and a pottery bowl of black beans.

I didn't know what Villa had ordered for himself and his officers, but I sat on the khaki blanket that served as a bedspread, happily gobbled everything, and could have used another portion of it all.

But within seconds of scraping the bowl, I leaned back against the flattened pillow, and when a knock sounded on the door and Eduardo's voice woke me, I realized I hadn't even taken off my boots.

"Cooper? It's nearly dawn."

"I'll be right there."

I hurriedly finger-combed my hair and brushed out my wrinkled dress, but there wasn't much I could do with either, and I took up Yolanda's straw hat again to leave the little bedroom.

When I got outside, Eduardo and General Villa waited for me. Eduardo looked sad, but not as sorrowful as he'd been the night before.

The general once more wore his brown pants, puttees, and sweater. He'd topped the outfit with a simple brown sombrero. Not a single decoration was pinned to the bulky sweater.

He smiled, and Eduardo translated, "Everything has been packed. Food and water and the f-film. Only one more thing has to go."

They both watched a bandit soldier come out with the white uniform and gold-braided officer's cap. As he folded it to go in the back of the pie wagon, I saw that all the medals and ribbons were still attached.

Eduardo said, "It was only on loan from the studio. M-Matt and I were supposed to bring it back."

"Venga." General Villa made the shooing motion to Eduardo and me, and we followed him to the pie wagon.

No soldiers stood guard around the house or the Tin Lizzie now, and only a few old men, women, and children wandered in the dawn of the little dirt square.

But where was Luther?

Had Villa reneged on our bargain despite his handshake? Did his smile in the morning light indicate a change of heart?

He still needed Eduardo to get the film back to Hollywood. And he obviously wanted Mars Studio to make the story of his life for the screen.

But he had everything I could give him from my grandfather.

The sky washed a cheerful pink, and gold flecked the clouds at the horizon.

The general motioned for Eduardo and me to get in the back of the truck.

But I didn't move.

"General Villa—" I began.

Then I saw two soldiers escorting Luther from the little hovel.

He staggered between the two bandits, barefoot in his grubby clothes and his filthy bandage, and obviously not used to walking on bare ground without shoes.

"How do you do, sir? " Eduardo made one of his courteous bows when Luther got close.

I wanted to tell him to stop it, but at least he didn't offer to shake hands, and I said to Villa. "You and my grandfather have met, haven't you, General?"

Villa smiled. "Por supuesto." Then he repeated, "Venga. We need to 1-leave right away."

'We?'

Villa obviously understood my glance and had Eduardo say, "I have decided to drive you to my hacienda. It is halfway to Juarez, and you can go on from there. I have sent a m-messenger ahead to alert my people that I am bringing guests. We shall leave immediately." He motioned again for me to climb in the back seat. "I will drive."

An orange rim of sun appeared over the horizon.

The man with gray hair who had brought us to the camp came up to Villa. They talked a moment while Eduardo offered his arm to help me onto the running board and then into the back seat.

I hesitated only a second before I took his hand.

He gave me a slight smile. But neither of us said anything as he, too, climbed into the back and sat down beside me.

He put Matt Gordon's gray hat over his dark hair.

Luther grappled awkwardly into the passenger seat as General Villa came up to the truck and slid behind the wheel.

He directed the gray-haired bandit to crank the motor, and the old man bent into the cranking with a laugh.

When the motor at last caught and hummed, the men around the square hooted and whistled with delight as if they hadn't witnessed the starting of a car before. They crowded in close to watch the hood vibrate.

The two women and Villa's little girls came from the adobe house.

Villa shouted something to them over the motor, yanked off the brake, and we moved away from the little huddle of houses and tents. The children waved good-bye.

General Villa had let Luther go as he'd promised.

We picked up speed.

But as the adobe houses and waving children, the tents and the forlorn cannons became swallowed into the dust of the truck, another apprehension struck me.

Suddenly I knew why Pancho Villa had decided to take us to his
hacienda before he let us drive on to Juarez and El Paso.

He didn't want to alienate President Wilson by publicly executing an American.

So he'd decided to kill Luther and me in the security of his own villa where no one would ever know.

25

Since Pancho Villa understood
English, I couldn't shout my apprehensions to Eduardo or Luther,
and I sat in the back seat, trying to keep my hands from trembling,
trying to look calmly at the general's thick neck under the rib of the
brown sweater, trying to plan as we whirled across the desiccated
landscape.

Villa followed his own road—or one from his imagination—
and we flew over the desert, and the pie wagon gathered more
speed until we barreled along at more than fifty miles an hour.

Villa would let Eduardo go unharmed. I could be certain about
that.

I couldn't imagine what excuse he'd give for having Luther and
me killed, but maybe he'd send Eduardo on alone, before he had us
shot, without apology. No one would ever find us buried in the
sand.

Luther squinted as the sun came up, raised himself in the passenger seat, looking as straight and as stern as he could, unshaven,
and in those dirty wrinkled clothes and wretched bandage.
Eduardo leaned back enough for the nape of his neck to brace
against the upright top of the seat. His handsome face under the
brim of the gray fedora once again sank into unhappiness as soon
as we left Aguas de los Caballos, and I knew there was nothing I
could say that would make him feel better about the loss of the

man he'd planned to watch out for, the man who had loved his
mother.

Nor could I say anything that would warn him about Pancho
Villa's plans for Luther and me.

I wondered if Villa would let us write a note to Angelica—and
Yolanda—before he had us executed.

I'd come so close to rescuing Luther.

I was no longer the innocent I'd been when I'd come to the
border, and now I could have made some changes in that sad
household back in El Paso.

But there was nothing I could do about that either, and I, too,
hunched sadly in the back seat.

Only General Villa seemed to be having a joyous time as he
pressed the accelerator up inclines and took his foot off the pedals
to coast, speeding down into the valleys again. He occasionally
turned and grinned from one of us to the other, but he didn't seem
to need an answering smile or a happy look from any of us as the
pie wagon zoomed along.

But then, perhaps Luther and I had done all we could do.

Maybe neither one of us was necessary any longer.

Since Angelica had to know about Yolanda's child and the casa
chica arrangement, she and Yolanda and the baby, whom Luther
and I would never see now, would have to take care of the store and
the diamonds.

I put my head back and tilted Yolanda's hat over my forehead.

Eduardo reached over and took my hand in his.

This time I didn't have an urge to shake him off.

I closed my eyes and decided that sometimes gallantry and
courtesy might be comforting.

His fingers pressed mine, and I pressed back. But I kept my eyes
shut.

For perhaps an hour.

When I opened my eyes again, I saw a barbed wire fence,

behind which a herd of Mexican long-horned cattle grazed on the
meager grass stubble between the sagebrush and mesquite.

We had to be coming to a hacienda.

Within another few minutes a more discernible road appeared. It ran beside a larger herd of cattle and a sturdier stretch of fencing, and maybe another half an hour more went by before a sprawling adobe house and dozens of out-buildings came into sight beyond the inadequate pasture land.

The two-story hacienda with its wrap-around porch loomed larger than the entire village we'd just left.

The general began to honk while he whirled the pie wagon onto a dirt driveway between two tall posts without slowing down. A wrought-iron V had been worked into the iron scroll over the posts.

Villa kept honking all the way to the house, and by the time we reached the front steps and the overhang of the tiles on the porch roof, a dozen adults—and even more children—stood on the verandah awaiting our arrival.

General Villa skidded the truck to a halt, drew on the brake, and leapt from beneath the steering wheel in one smooth movement as if he were jumping off the back of a barely reined-in horse.

Peasants in white cotton clothes hurried down the steps, and the women and children scrambled off the porch at once. Everyone surrounded the general.

He smiled and laughed, talking to everyone at once, as he went up the steps with the crowd around him. At the door he turned and gestured to us to get out of the pie wagon and come inside with him.

Well, at least the peasants—whom I knew doubled as soldiers when Villa needed them—hadn't pulled out rifles yet.

The rest of the crowd made the picture of a harmless family group. They weren't what I'd been expecting.

"General Villa wants us to go inside with him," Luther said—as if Eduardo and I hadn't noticed.

But neither of us objected. Eduardo released my hand and took my elbow as we climbed stiffly and grittily from the back seat. Luther got down from the passenger side.

He looked old and tired in the soiled shirt, bandage, and bare feet.

We went up to the porch together.

As General Villa disappeared inside the house, the line of children came out again to stand and stare at us. There were a score of them.

Perhaps the general wouldn't kill us in the presence of so many of his children.

The entryway was cool, and the women had gathered on the polished tiles to watch us file inside.

Villa stopped at the dining room doorway and made an announcement. I moved aside for Eduardo to come forward. Luther could have translated, but I was used to Eduardo, and I could see that Villa liked the young actor better than he liked Luther.

The general beamed at us all as he completed the long welcoming speech and swept his arm wide to indicate his boundless hospitality.

"My servants always have ice cream for me when I return h-home," he said grandly. "You must have a dish with me before you set out for El Paso."

I wondered if he might be going to poison Luther and me.

And, of course, our sickness would be enough excuse to send Eduardo on to El Paso without us. Later, if anyone got curious—perhaps General Pershing—Villa could merely send word that we hadn't recovered.

But Villa was beaming as he led us into a dining room full of sunlight and air from the open square windows.

He directed us all to sit down with him at the table.

The children vanished, and two women pattered into the room from the kitchen, one with glasses of water and silver spoons, the other with crystal dishes. Each dish held a scoop of vanilla ice cream.

I watched the woman with the ice cream closely, but I couldn't see that she made any distinction between the dishes or that she placed a special one before Villa or before either me or Luther.

Villa made his grand gesture of hospitality again, gave another long welcoming speech while the cream puddled in the crystal dishes. Finally he picked up his spoon.

"Eat, eat," he said. "The cream has been tasted by my wife in the kitchen. And you are my guests. My guests have n-nothing to fear under my roof."

I hoped that was true.

26

THE ICE CREAM was cool, smooth, and I
couldn't taste the acrid flavor of a drug or a poison. And although
Luther seemed to have trouble eating with his left hand, we all finished the ice cream in a matter of minutes.

I was still afraid Villa might think of another delay, and I said
with prompt finality as I put down my spoon, "You've been most
kind, General Villa. That was a wonderful treat."

Luther started. He stared at me as if my speaking to the general
had been totally unexpected and uncalled for.

I'd forgotten he didn't know Villa and I had been speaking—
through Eduardo—for the last two days. I'd forgotten Luther didn't
know that Villa liked spirit.

And, of course, Villa didn't look shocked at all.

He merely smiled and made another gracious flowery speech.

We all three nodded, but before there could be any speechmaking on the part of either Luther or Eduardo, I said, "I am most
grateful for your thoughtfulness and for your driving us as far as
your hacienda." I stood up, and Luther gaped at that, too. "But I
think we need to leave for El Paso as soon as we can. I want to
arrange for my grandfather to see a doctor as soon as possible, and
I won't know the way if we have to travel in the dark."

"Por supuesto, Señorita."

He pushed back his chair and got up at once. "I had my men
put more gasoline into your truck. I have my own s-supply."

Then he led the way back outside.

The dusty pie wagon sat at the foot of the porch steps.

Villa stopped in the shade and explained with expansive gestures to Eduardo how to get to the railroad tracks and the road that would lead to El Paso. Then he called one of the peasants, took the man's straw sombrero, and presented it to Luther with a bow.

And after a few more speeches, we were climbing into the truck again.

I got behind the wheel and Eduardo pulled on Matt Gordon's hat as he climbed in the back to let Luther have the passenger seat.

"We'll hit a fork in the road just beyond the end of his land. Take the one to the left," Eduardo said from behind me.

I looked up at the general still standing on his porch. "Thank you again, General Villa."

"You are welcome, Señorita. You see, I am not a man with two faces."

He motioned to the waiting peasant who'd given up his hat to Luther. The man hurried over to turn the crank, and the motor started more smoothly than I'd ever heard it start before.

"Good-bye, Señores, Señorita," Pancho Villa shouted in heavily accented English as he waved.

I waved back as we pulled away from the house and the crowd surrounding the stout man in the brown sweater.

I'd guessed wrong again. Thank heavens.

The last thing I saw of the general was his broad smile around the jagged yellow teeth. Then the house disappeared into the dust.

We reached the end of the barbed wire fence, turned left at the fork, and within a few more minutes I could see railroad tracks and telegraph lines ahead.

We turned left again, speeding back the way we'd come from Juarez.

It was hard to believe, but we were actually heading for El Paso.

Eduardo leaned forward. "I need to s-send a wire as soon as we arrive."

I nodded through the swirl of dust.

"You're driving too fast over this dirt road," Luther shouted, holding onto the straw hat.

I didn't slow down.

"As soon as we cross the river, I'll take you to the hospital," I shouted back. "Just tell me how to find it. You can get gangrene from a wound like that."

Then I said, "I've decided to have Yolanda move all that furniture out of the rooms on the third floor so she can have one as her bedroom, and we can use one as a nursery."

"Don't try to meddle! I wanted you to take care of Yolanda if Villa executed me. But he didn't. Now I can take care of things. Yolanda and her baby are none of your concern."

"Lo siento!" I yelled over the sound of the motor. "My new uncle or aunt is my business, and there's nothing you can do about it."

I pressed the accelerator pedal.

"I'm going to open the drapes. Angelica will just have to learn to live with the light."

"You don't understand."

"Of course I don't. All I can do is try. But no one is going to raise our new baby in a casa chica or in the dark."

Luther looked at me from under the peasant straw hat that looked rather rakish on him. I saw him try to frown as his lips moved with the words, "Just like Alex," but at the same time I caught a glimpse of the approval on his face before he turned away to stare at the railroad track speeding along beside us.

$\mathcal{P}$AT CARR has taught English at Rice, Tulane, and the University of New Orleans. She is the author of five novels, three nonfiction titles, and four book-length short story collections. She lives in Elkins, Arkansas.